The Bride's Undoing

Ashly Senger

Contents

Prologue

He stood before, caressed my ring with a gentle, sad smile.

"I am sorry..."

A tear rolled down my cheeks, as my bridal attire weighed down on me. It was raining heavily, and I was standing at the corner of the street, watching my newly-attained husband crush my heart in the most brutal ways.

We had driven here straight from the wedding hall.

"Was it all a lie?" My makeup was already ruined by the rain, and the tears were ruining it further. The night sky was cloudy, and there were hardly any people around me.

Eliyas and I had just got married.

After our marriage, he had headed out with a convenient apology and a resigned look, causing me to run after him in a desperate and panicked way.

"Shhhh..." He tipped my chin, wiping some of my tears with his thumb, not caring as it further smudged my make-up.

"I was warned-d..." I revealed, hiccuping, crying in a pitiful and deeply hurt man. "I was w-warned, yet I chose you." I sobbed, resting my cheek against the palm that he now had cupped around my face.

"I am sorry."

I closed my eyes in pain.

"Please stay..." I opened them again, watching as his hair swayed with the cool wind, his luminous eyes seemed shiny under the dazzling weather.

"I can't. You know how this was going to be. Deep down, I know you knew that this wasn't meant to be. I am sorry. For what it is worth, conning you has crushed me too, but as I have always said...not everyone gets what they want. Goodbye, princess." He gently patted my head and then walked away.

He had chosen to just walk away from my tears. He had just watched my ruination and walked away. Taking away my wealth, the naive and dreamy spark of my life, he had just walked away.

He had just stood, felt my heartbreaking pain and took in my torture like it soothed his heart. Deep down, I knew that our story had been too dream-like to be true. I knew that his love might have a heavy price. A rugged bad-boy biker with rings on his fingers and charm as his talent. I knew nothing about my bookish and nerdy ways seemed adventurous to him, yet he had been such a beautiful lie.

Now that he was leaving, I wanted to chase after him, beg him to not leave me abandoned, force him to teach me the art of forgetting too. I wanted sweet lies, him to spare me just another glance, see the damage he had done. Yet, I was offered nothing.

With the plane tickets in his hands, it was obvious he was now only going to be just a devastating illusion in my mind.

Dressed as a bride under the bright moonlight, I had been left behind with life-long scars, trauma and hurt.

This was the first stroke of naive hearts' ruination.

Chapter 1

Sila

It started as a glorious fairytale. I used to catch a bus to my college with my cousins, and a biker seemed to have got charmed by my presence. The loud, sneaky laughter of his friends, them elbowing each other whenever I walked past them on my way to my college, him choosing me over my cousins...the sensation was dizzily warm.

He was bold, confident and sweet, so openly announced his affiliations. I was an insecure, shy girl who had hardly ever heard words of praise.

I was easy prey.

While walking back from college one day, he had stopped and just simply proposed in front of everyone. We had never exchanged even words before that. His bold, straightforward approach had been so surprising, so shocking yet so flattering. My own insecurities and desperation to be more than just a book nerd, invisible in crowds, had been my own doom.

"Marry me." The twinkle in his stance, the sincerity in his words... he had proposed with a diamond ring. My cousins had immediately ganged up on him for being so obscene and immediately walked me away from the dark streets of Mahal Road. I wish I had never looked back at the words of the street charmer again, yet I did.

"I like someone, mama," I shyly spoke, playing with my fingers.

We lived in a joint family, so openly making such declarations in front of the whole family could be met with a lot of disapproval. I had pulled my mother from our kitchen and into my room. Before my cousins could tell my mother anything, I wanted to be the first one to share my liking with her.

Her eyes rounded with surprise, though I was not sure if this was pleasant or tormented. "Where? How? Do I know him?" She sat beside me on the bed. I had purposely kept the lights of my room dim to feign a feeling of secrecy.

"Maybe..." I shyly tucked a loose hair lock behind my ear while momentarily staring at the cushion placed on my legs and picking on its beads. "He has been liking me for some time. And-"

"Is he the biker boy?" My mom interrupted, with a serious and sombre look this time. She had folded her hands.

"How did you know?" I gasped, snapping my head in her direction.

"Your cousins told their mums about how the infamous street boy has been stalking all of you, and how he tends to follow you around." There was an element of disapproval, disappointment lining her tone.

"Y-yes, but h-he is a v-very nice guy." I knew it was time to plead my case. Cheeks rounded with the preparation of all that I had wanted to say, express the fluttering in my heart caused by the street boy liking me.

"Sila, he wears rings and is mostly found on the streets. The air guns you hear at night...it is him and his friends. He is not a good man, my dear. Boys from the streets never are. He has no job, can offer no stability, and I am extremely furious about how he has been stalking my baby girl. I thought you were smarter than this, Sila." She reprimanded.

I straightened up in my defence. "How can you say that mama...I am an adult. I think you have taught me well enough to know what is good or bad for me. And he...he is a good person. Weren't you the one always telling me to never judge a book by its cover. He is sweet. He never ever made me feel uncomfortable and was a fine gentleman in my presence.

I know he has a rough exterior, but I know his heart is good. He respects me. That is what I want in my husband; to have a good heart and really like me."

"Sweetie," she gently patted my head. "We will find a good man for you, but not him, Sila." There was a sternness in her tone. "He doesn't have a good background. You have no idea about his family, lifestyle...all we see him do is roam around on our streets with his friends on black bikes and terrorize people."

"He never terrorized-"

"The way these youngsters zoom around our town is 'terrorizing'." She pressed.

I sighed with exhaustion, lowering my gaze to my hands.

I knew convincing my mom about any of this would be difficult. She and my pa had always made sure that I had a protected and sheltered life. I was their little baby, yet I wanted to experience going with my heart for once.

Eliyas, the biker man, made my heart flutter. He was so tall, charming and had this bad-boyish vibe that spoke of a good heart entrapped underneath his rough exterior. Though his straightforwardness was unnecessary, he was a confident alpha man.

I was just a shy book-reader who hardly knew anything about this world. I was tired of my ugly thick-rim glasses, hated myself for being a doormat for many of my peers and wanted to compete with the social butterfly versions of my cousins. In fact, I had been fortunate to have such a ruggedly strong man choose me among all of my cousins.

"He proposed to me today...mama," I revealed after a moment of silence, staring at my fidgeting fingers with a bit of sadness.

"What the heck! This is how he is respecting you, Sila!" Fury gripped her immediately. "That is it. That boy is upto no good stalking and countering our girl in this manner. I will talk to your pa. He needs to be reported for this." She sharply got up, making me immediately tug on her hand in panic and horror.

"No, please, mama. It is alright." I pleaded. "He won't bother me again. Please...I will make sure of it!" I began to cry, only for her to immediately pull me into a hug.

"Shhh...okay, I won't tell your pa," she tenderly assured. "You know sweetie I love you so much, and I just don't want anyone to hurt you. You are sweet, naive and my little baby. I don't ever want anyone to hurt your heart." The hug tightened.

"I love you too, mama." I hugged her back, not telling her that my heart was already broken by not being supported while making my own choices.

The next morning, I got up early and walked alone to the bus stop. My cousins had their classes at different timings, and after a night full of words to never speak of Eliyas again, my mother had allowed me to go on my own. I guess it was her way of psychologically portraying that she trusted me.

With my head lowered and arms wrapped around my books, I walked until I reached the infamous street where it had all begun. My heart hurt going down there, but there was no other route. The feeling of wanting something, yet knowing that I didn't have a choice but to let go, hurt.

The sound of male laughter and casual smiles echoed in the other. Mum's yesterday's words clicked in my mind.

Yes, what did Eliyas do?

However, just as I stepped on the gravel road of Mahal Street, the whispers settled down.

"Oe, she is here!" Someone spoke.

I just kept my gaze lowered, face hidden and kept on walking.

Nerves and shyness hit me hard as I passed Eliyas, while his group was standing, leaning against the dirty wall and telephone booths of the street.

Silence echoed for a moment. I could feel attention focus on me, making it more difficult to walk without tripping. Blush filled my cheeks, as mute whispers began echoing in the air. They were talking about me.

"Sila," Eliyas suddenly called up, his feet now jogging in my direction.

I panicked and fastened my steps.

"Wait!" He tried to stop me.

"Umm...I just wanted to ask what is your answer?" The confident male sounded hesitant for a second. I momentarily paused, my back towards him, hurt and pain filling up my nerves. It was a yes, but it had to be no. I closed my eyes as I listened.

"If it is a no, I won't bother you again...ever! But hear me out before you say anything..." There was desperation in his tone. "I am 28 years old. I have a small family that lives in Karachi. I live here with my brothers in a 1 story house. I admit my job isn't anything out of the ordinary, but I work as an evening salesperson at a mobile shop. If you say yes, I promise I will keep you happy. I will keep loving you and will have my family fly here from Karachi to meet your folks."

I didn't know what to say.

I wanted to turn around and tell him that I had no issues. My nerves were completely twisted out of shyness, but I couldn't do anything about it. My silence made him desperate to convince me.

"Please...I know I don't have a good reputation on these streets. My brothers and I are mostly loud brats and pass our time here. But my brothers, my friends, we are all good people. We never hurt anyone." A snicker from behind him echoed out suddenly, but Eliyas completely ignored it. "My family already knows about you. I admit I can be compulsive, sensitive and an overthinking brat sometimes. My temper gets fumed and my rough biker attitude puts people off, but I truly do adore you. You are a good girl, I can tell. You belong to a good family, and I don't want to discomfort you in any way. Just give me a chance..."

"O-okay."

My heart had finally spoken. His words, promises had been so much. A man wanting to marry me with such desperation, his emotions so sincere and warm, I would be a fool to ignore it. Sincere love was hardly ever found. A person who truly cares about you without knowing you, or hearing your words shouldn't be let go.

I had been so naive.

Weeks passed with him secretly dropping off gifts, cards for me. His affectionate gifts were so heartwarming, flattering...his family even flew here from Karachi, and I secretly got to meet his mum, but I had no idea how this was going to work. My family was never going to approve.

My anxiety and stress grew when my parents suddenly started to look for a match for me. I felt so trapped, so hurt...I knew they weren't going to listen to me. I decided to talk about this issue with Eliyas's mother. She would know what to do.

On my way from college, I headed to Eliyas's family house. The mother was quick to greet me at the entrance while holding a little sleeping baby in her hands. 'My nephew' she had introduced.

The little boy was so cute, with chubby cheeks. I never knew that one of Eliyas's brothers was married...the baby made their whole family seem so homely.

"We can sit in the garden."

'Sure." I smiled

We sat on white metal chairs in the small garden, feeling the wind blowing in our faces. Eliyas's family house wasn't painted from the outside, but it was well-kept and had pink flower vines covering some of its greyness. It was like a local, domesticated cottage.

"So, when are we finally going to make you our daughter-in-law? She joked, caressing the little boy's hair. The baby yawned in his sleep and wrapped his hand around her fingers.

Awww...so cute!

"Umm...I wanted to talk about that..." I drawled. Eliyas's mum was a tall, wise-looking lady. Her hair showed age, her hands showed hard work and her fists showed authority, so I naturally felt intimidated in her presence. Yet, she had also been so warm and welcoming towards me that it relaxed my nerves.

'My dear, what is wrong?" she spoke with concern and curiosity in her gaze.

"My family doesn't approve of this," I confessed with my head low, feeling ashamed of saying this directly, but this was the truth. I wanted them to be clear about this.

"Oh, don't worry. We will come and visit them-"

"No!" I immediately panicked, waving my hands frantically. "I live in a joint family. This will lead to a lot of questions and fingers. I can't have that. Also, my parents will never approve. They have already started looking for potential husbands for me."

"Does Eliyas know of this?" She frowned.

I looked away. "I don't know."

"Hmm...don't worry, my dear. You are a wonderful girl. My Eliyas loves you a lot, and I know that he won't let you go so easily. In fact, we already consider you as our family. I am pretty sure we will find a way out of this. Now since you are here, I would love for you to have tea with me."

"Sure," I smiled, feeling relaxed yet worried.

What if Eliyas thought this was all not worth the effort?

However, days passed...and soon, on my way to the bus stop, I was confronted by Eliyas again on one extremely cloudy day. This time, none of his friends were with him.

"Sila, run away with me." His voice had held so much earnestness and promises.

My lowered eyes widened in shock.

"Look...I know your family doesn't approve, but I can't have you be anyone else's. My family is here. We can have a small marriage ceremony and then tell your family. Once they see how happy you are, how I will take care of you...they will approve. You are the most beautiful girl I have ever seen, and I am not ever going to give up this easily. I will always fight for you." His promises, praise and vows made my heart flutter so much.

What he was saying sounded insane. My family had to attend my wedding. Yet, crazily, this made sense too. After my marriage, I could prove to my family that I was right about Eliyas. Once they saw how good he was to me, they would definitely approve. They loved me.

I would make up for this hurt by apologizing, begging for their forgiveness and working my best to please them in any way possible. I would apologize to my entire joint family. Though they were judgemental, if they saw me well-settled and happy, their fingers would lower.

Then, I would have a grand wedding ceremony with them.

This was beyond something I could even think of doing, so unfamiliar with my personality, yet being in love does that.

My heart was racing with this new, highly risky arrangement.

This was insane!

Something in my silence was a good enough answer for him.

"Okay, yes! I will borrow some cash from my friends for our wedding ceremony. Don't worry, I will work consecutive extra shifts to pay it off...but right now, we need that money, and you are worth it!."

This made me feel so bad.

He was willing to do so much for me, work hard...and I was only bringing him more trouble. The feeling of guilt was so heavy that I decided to contribute.

This was our marriage.

I would sell the jewellery my mom had gifted me and wanted me to wear on my wedding day. I would sell some of my personal favourite gold stashes...and I did.

After gathering the money, I informed Eliyas's mother that I had arranged for the cash and would give it to him on our wedding day so that he could pay back the loans immediately.

It had been such a fool-proof trap that I had no idea how easy it had been to manipulate me.

I had been completely fooled by a rough biker.

Chapter 2

S ila

There are moments when even your strength echoes a deep cry of loneliness. Choosing Eliyas was an unconscious cry of loneliness...suppressed hurt of always staying in the background. For once, I wanted to somehow match up with my cousins. The shy me wanted to reach out to others but just didn't know how.

Eliyas seemed like a dream come true, which took me away from the insecurity of being left behind. I had been trailing behind. I just wanted a hand to grip to pull me along, treat me as I mattered, and Eliyas did that. I didn't have much of a voice among my cousins, but with Eliyas, it felt like my presence mattered so much.

I was tired of always chasing after the feeling of being treated important while beingtaken for granted by my party-going cousins. We lived together, so there were plans made. I would often be kept out of those plans. This wasn't purposely leaving me out of stuff. I just held the reputation of being happy with my books and isolation. In fact, my shyness had more like labelled my interests. I didn't fit in...so I was better left out.

Eliyas's attention made me feel so special, belonged and giddy. It was such a fortune of mine that I forgot to weigh its cost. It was the feeling of first love...that heart stopping emotion that just makes you leap. One never looks for the consequences, because those first promises always hit the hardest. Being sensitive, it was easy for me to get obsessed, become super loyal and insanely attached.

I had found the gushy tale people chased after.

I had been gifted such a man.

My wedding day was a mixture of giddy emotions. I had secretly transferred my stuff to Eliyas's family house a day before and the cash, too. His mother had taken me to a private parlour for makeup, and I guess that should have been the first clue. While getting me ready, his mother had hardly even looked busy.

"Isn't she gorgeous?" My face had been pushed before a mirror at the parlour, while I smiled at my to-be mother-in-law's sweet words. The make-up artist just smiled.

"True. Your son is a lucky man."

"He is smart." The strange silence in her tone never strung me in the wrong way. Maybe, because I was just high up on cloud nine, so happy and giddy about my marriage. The elated emotions of marrying Eliyas were dizzily mesmerizing. A bad-boy biker with power, charm and confidence had chosen me.

Beautiful...he had made me feel beautiful.

My wedding dress was royal blue. And I was gifted two golden bracelets to adorn with them by my mother-in-law. Nora told me that she had those bracelets gifted to her by Eliyas's grandmother and was now passing them on.

Such a sentimental trap.

I felt guilt for doing this behind my family's back, for not including them in anything right now, but they just didn't understand. Eliyas made me feel happy, confident and beautiful. I would go back to them after proving that this was what I wanted, that I had, for once, fought for myself. I never did that before. No demands, requests, anything...I never said no.

The parlour was situated in a rusty old building on our neighbouring street. I had left home, and I knew chaos was to begin soon, my search was to begin soon, but before a lot of fingers could raise, I had promised myself that I would go back with new-found strength. My strength and newly gained status would be enough to sway away from the fingers. After all, a married woman in this society had a voice.

Anyhow, after getting my makeup done, Nora had escorted me to a cheap yellow taxi. This should have been the second clue. I wasn't been protected in any way. I was caked up for the show. Yet, I had only focused on Eliyas's love. My own feeling of adoration. Never believe that it would lead to ruination.

The rainy clouds had started echoing in the air. And through some suspicious streets, I had been driven to the wedding hall, which was located near the outskirts of my city. The taxi driver was an old man. Nora...she didn't speak a single word on the way to the hall. I thought it was my nerves that had drowned out her words, but later late-night reminiscing had confirmed that she had been very cold.

Nervous while staring at the passing stress, watching elite roads turn muddy and get lined by trees and scrubs, I kept on silently driving to the wedding arena, wondering how Eliyas would react to my arrival. However, upon reaching the arena, which seemed more of an abandoned warehouse than a hall, I had conveniently understood that Eliyas had money problems, but it didn't matter to me. Together, we would manage.

This was my compromise, my show of affection, dedication and loyalty.

Money didn't sway my affection.

Feeling super excited and nervous, I was helped out of the car with the help of Nora. The taxi had stopped right in front of the grey building of the wedding hall. There were greasy factories in the faraway distance, brown grass and scrubs outlining the hall. The place was located in a rather deserted area...

My jewellery had been worth much more than that.

Upon stepping inside the hall, I found out that Eliyas was already there with the witness.

So this was really happening.

"You ready, my dear..." Nora began escorting me to one of the hall's rooms going down from the main hall in which Eliyas was sitting there with some men.

"I am." I shyly nodded, making sure to not trip over.

"My Eliyas couldn't take his eyes off you," she teased, making me blush with so much delight.

"He really loves you. And he is such a fortunate man to get such a wonderful woman." She side-hugged me. I only blushed harder. The giddy emotion was worth it.

The corridor was hardly lit by a white light.

There were rooms with open doors on both sides and strange scents breathing out of them. Not minding, I was escorted to the room on the furthest, at the rear end of the hall.

Upon opening the wooden door of that room, Nora had turned on the lights and coaxed me to step in.

Inside, there was just a brown couch pressed against the wall, a chair and a table. There were no windows and the ceiling fan seemed to be too dangerous to be turned on. Nothing mattered to me.

"Settle down, my dear...." I took the chair while Nora took the couch.

Now it was time to wait.

Married.

Immediately after getting married, I had beamed at Nora would so much delight, moving to hug her, only to have her look at me with a strange gleam of satisfaction. There was no motherly happiness. Her lack of emotion was finally able to click my instincts.

Something was wrong here.

Something very wrong was happening...

"Nora, is everything alright?'

"I will be right back." She had simply shrugged.

She never did get back.

Eliyas was the only one to later fool me again by claiming how happy he was and announce that it was time to drive me back home. My hand gripped and guarded, he had so gently escorted me to a black car parked outside. He had suddenly felt like my protective shield, rejoiced that his dream had come true. Mine, too.

The drive back home, however, soon started confirming my intuition. The happy and talkative Eliyas soon morphed into a silent man as he drove us down the dark sky. The pouring rain worried my heart more as I wondered about his sudden shift in mood.

This was not what I had expected.

He didn't spare me a glance, as he held the steering wheel with both his arms and began driving at a fast speed.

"What about Nora?" I shared a hesitant glance in his direction, feeling my wedding attire suddenly so heavy and drowning. The leather seats of the car no longer seemed big enough.

My words only got ignored by him, making me feel tiny and stare at my fidgeting fingers.

I couldn't understand why he was acting like this...

Until we stopped in the midst of some dirty old street.

"Get out."

My horrors had been confirmed.

He stood before, caressed my ring with a gentle, sad smile.

"I am sorry..."

A tear rolled down my cheeks, as my bridal attire weighed down on me. It was raining heavily, and I was standing at the corner of the street, watching my newly-attained husband crush my heart in the most brutal ways. Confessions had been made.

We had driven here straight from the wedding hall, only for reality to struck me hard.

"Was it all a lie?" My makeup was already ruined by the rain, and the tears were ruining it further. The night sky was cloudy, and there were hardly any people around me.

Eliyas and I had just got married.

This had just been the beginning of the chapter for me.

How could he stoop so low?

After our marriage getaway, him simply ordering me out of his car and dropping me off before a closed shop while offering to make a phone call for me later, he had headed out with a convenient apology and a resigned look, causing me to run after him in a desperate and panicked way.

"Shhhh..." He tipped my chin, wiping some of my tears with his thumb, not caring as it further smudged my make-up.

"I was warned-d..." I revealed, hiccuping, crying in a pitiful and deeply hurt man. "I was w-warned, yet I chose you." I sobbed, resting my cheek against the palm that he now had cupped around my face.

"I am sorry."

I closed my eyes in pain.

"Please stay..." I opened them again, watching as his hair swayed with the cool wind, his luminous eyes seemed shiny under the dazzling weather.

"I can't. You know how this was going to be. Deep down, I know you knew that this wasn't meant to be. I am sorry. For what it is worth, conning you have crushed me too, but as I have always said...not everyone gets what they want. Goodbye, princess." He gently patted my head and then walked away.

Finally, I was seeing him for the man he was. The ugly side of his personality my mom had warned me about, his true street-rough nature, was clear. The tears collected in my eyes, the whimpering sensation and the piercing sharp sound of a heart being crush haunted me.

He had chosen to just walk away from my tears. He had just watched my ruination and walked away. Taking away my wealth, the naive and dreamy spark of my life, he had just walked away.

He had just stood, felt my heartbreaking pain and took in my torture like it soothed his heart. And it destroyed me to think that he had been right with some of his words. Deep down, I knew that our story had been too dream-like to be true. I knew that his love might have a heavy price. A rugged bad-boy biker with rings on his fingers and charm as his talent. I knew nothing about my bookish and nerdy ways seemed adventurous to him, yet he had been such a beautiful lie.

Now that he was leaving, I wanted to chase after him, beg him to not leave me abandoned, force him to teach me the art of forgetting too. I wanted sweet lies, him to spare me just another glance, see the damage he had done. Yet, I was offered nothing.

With the plane tickets in his hands, it was obvious he was now only going to be just a devastating illusion in my mind. He had played his part, his wicked scheme. It was time to move on.

Settling back in his car, he had simply driven away, not bothering that he had left me alone and unsafe in a suspicious place...not wondering how a simple girl, who had never done him wrong, was going to pay for his cruelty.

Dressed as a bride under the bright moonlight hidden by the dark rainy clouds, I had been left behind with life-long scars, trauma and hurt. The horror of what just had happened to me sank in, and I soon collapsed on the floor....my nerves making me lose my consciousness.

This was the first stroke of naive hearts' ruination.

Chapter 3

One year later

Eliyas

Smiling his pearl whites, visibly noticing the girl charmed by his looks, Eliyas slowly grabbed the cash from her hands.

"Thank you, dear. I-I don't know what to say. This doesn't feel right." He feigned a rather hesitant and embarrassed look, scratching his neck. "After our wedding, I will pay it back. I will work double shifts. I will take another job. For you, I-"

"Hush," The girl stopped him with a fond smile. "It is okay. I know you will." The trust and naivety in her eyes almost made Eliyas smirk in amusement, but he hid his emotions well simply by giving the girl a sharp nod.

Gullible...Miss Jasmine was a fashion diva, the clever head girl of her university and a social butterfly, but she had been such easy prey. She was admired and adored, yet her fascination with danger and her interest in bad boys had been her doom.

Dummy!

Feeling the stack of money in his hands, which the pretty diva had pulled out from her designer bag, Eliyas simply gave his admirer an intensely sweet smile and turned around to walk out of the alley where he had just conned a rich brat.

Brains didn't always equal popularity.

Not all rich borns deserved silver spoons.

Miss Jasmine had been so desperately eager when he had asked her to meet him in the alley behind her university. The young girl had welcomed him with a giddy smile and listened to his promises with so much hope. She was spoiled, rich and bratty but seemed to have no issues trusting Eliyas.

Eliyas adored such victims. It was fun ruffling their feathers and seeing how even their wealth couldn't stop them from being so easily manipulated by the poor. The settled feeling of seeing them turn so desperate and naive for his charms was wholesome...promising.

A dirty biker boy had made rich sophisticated women fall so easily for him.

Leaving Jasmine alone in the dark shadows, not even offering to drop her home, Eliyas ruffled his hair with an arrogant smile and walked towards a tinted window Cultus parked just around the corner.

Another girl's pretty little dreams ruined...

More cash in...

"Let's go." He roughly pulled open the door and slide onto the passenger seat.

"How much did she give?" Saud, his best friend, spoke from the passenger seat.

Eliyas pushed back his seat and laid down with a satisfied smile, placing an arm over his eyes to block out the sunlight. "A couple of guards, enough to get out of this town and finally get employed as a project manager for Kingsburg inc in Hill land," he nonchalantly spoke, breathing in the comfort of the ride and allowing it to cradle him into a relaxed mood.

It was a sunny day, a cosy afternoon...

"That is good to hear," Saud snickered, eyeing his friend in an impressed manner. It was pretty hard conning billionaires, but Eliyas had made it seem so easy.

"We can book tickets for Thursday. We will meet in the basement tonight for preparations. I want my cut before we go," Saud then began instructing in a business-like manner.

This was the routine protocol.

Every time they conned, they ran away. However, this time, Hill land was going to be a place where they finally settled down. It was going to be something out of the norm, but Eliyas had been stern about wanting to get some white-collar job; his son needed some consistency in life, and they had been too bold recently with their schemes.

"Whatever..." Eliyas shrugged, a yawn escaping.

Little Nabeel randomly laughed from behind. The baby had been strapped onto a baby seat placed on the backseat of the car and was given a dirty rubber toy to chew on. He was usually a quiet child, but his father's voice always made him laugh in adoration.

Feeling tender, Eliyas simply reached back and pulled on his son's cheek. His baby was his world. He would crush anyone who even dared harm the hair of his son. He was always too willing to bash a few bones.

"Though," Saud mused, as he got the car on drive mode, "If you would have just married Jasmine, you would have become rich. We could have made a fortune for some time- until she caught up. That woman would have made you the CEO of her father's company."

"But I am already married." Eliyas feigned a gasp in mock-offence, turning around to give his friend a dirty grin, mischief clear in his eyes. "My wife won't like me bringing home another," he mused. Clear dark humour was there.

"You are nasty." Slapping Eliyas on the arm in a playful manner, Saud pressed the accelerator.

It was a pleasure doing business with Eliyas.

The basement was where all the dirty thieves, mafia, gangs, con-men, corrupt businessmen, politicians, crooks and street criminals gathered, relaxed and traded. Everyone took part in deals. It was branched out to so many countries, a place notorious for being a highly illegal dark market, and was situated in the shadiest areas.

Now with dark smoke lingering in the air and the smell of malicious intents echoing from all corners, Eliyas stood inside one of the shabby warehouses of the basement, punching a box bag with his hands taped, his mood relaxed and his back facing the exit door.

The midnight clock had just struck...

Around him, there was just the eerie smell of oil, grease, gun powder and smoke. The only source of light in the room was the dull-ceiling bulb hanging above a table placed in one corner of the room. Stacks of loose cash had been piled up on the table along with some packets of gun powder. Also, two heavy bikes were parked inside the room, right next to the main door. The floor was too grey, stony, rough and half covered by a dirty brown carpet to be taken care of.

Saud was sitting on a dirty mattress pressed against the wall, on the right side of Eliyas, and was feeling a sleepy Nabeel a half-filled bottle of milk. The room was quiet, with occasional gunshots and screams echoing from the market outside.

Murders and human trafficking sales were common here.

"You should have given me a bigger cut." Saud mused, leaning against the wall, as Eliyas hit the boxing bag, again and again, flexing his muscles to express his power and control. Focus, he needed that.

"The females were greedy. They didn't settle for any less than one grand. Be glad, you got this much. I will get us more in Hill land." Eliyas struck the bag again. He had been exercising for an hour, but the sweat was worth staying in command and control. He couldn't help hitting out every ounce of his frustration and irritation for calmness. He enjoyed exhaustion, a mind too tired and exercised to focus on any idle thought. Extreme aching muscles feel like a soothing ointment to him.

"We could have made a profit if we just had sold the women. I heard Suraj made a fortune out of selling some farm girls. We could have done the same..."

"Too risky. Suraj spent two years in jail for that." Eliyas rubbed his knuckles in preparation to strike again, as he slightly hopped around the boxing bag with furrowed eyebrows, mood serious and bored.

"Yes, but we could have easily sold Sila. She was too naive and stupid. She had chosen to run away with you. She became your wife. We could have easily brought her here. I heard the Viper gang digs selling that kind of women-innocent and easily moldable. Your wife could have made us millionaires instead of just owners of her rusty jewellery sets."

"She is still my wife." A malicious smile appeared on Eliyas's face, as he met his friend gaze with a dark gleam in his eyes."So, maybe, we still have a chance to earn more." He offered, rubbing his thumb against his jaw in thought.

Sila...it had been a year...

"Yeah right. As if...you spared her once. I know you will spare her again," Saud scoffed with a roll of his eyes, cradling Nabeel and placing him down on the dirty mattress. The baby was the only soul still left untainted in this place. Eliyas was going to make sure it stayed that way.

"Did he finish his milk?" Eliyas changed the topic, eyeing his son with a sense of pride and fondness.

"Nope. Fell asleep before that." Saud tenderly patted away Nabeel's lock away from his forehead. The baby deserved better than a dirty mattress. It was a good thing they were moving to the Hill land.

"Okay. I will take care of him." Eliyas finally moved away from the boxing bag, wiping his face with a greasy towel and then hanging that towel around his neck. He was in sheer comfort mode.

Quickly swooping Nabeel into his arms and relaxing his muscles to become gentle for his baby, he sat down on the mattress, next to Saud, and leaned against the wall.

The exhaustion of the day made him close his eyes.

"I am going to go and buy us some more guns. I heard some real cheap guns from Europe have just been imported here. I will go and check if the rumour is true."

"Okay. But you will buy them with your share." This was business. Even though Saud had been his closest friend, money was never a negotiation between them.

With a muted pause, Saud finally nodded. "Okay."

Listening to Saud get up and step out of the room, Eliyas opened his eyes again and absently peered down at his baby. Caressing the cheek of Nabeel, he smiled with warm emotion.

Hill land...he hoped his son would achieve all that his father had never been able to.

Sila

The dizzy lights of the city. The usual flowing of my tears as they soiled my pillows at night and broke my heart, over and over again, was a constant ache inside me. Regrets, terrified, scarred, mentally shattered, I had experienced it all...was experiencing it all.

The ultimate betrayal of my life had ruined me. The night I had been discarded on the open streets as a married woman had been torturous. It was a dark memory that would give me so many night-mares, making me wake up and realize that my nightmarish hurt was my reality.

I had fallen for the most obvious scams.

The horror of waking up in the middle of nowhere, realizing I had nowhere to go and finding some dangerous, creepy street men hov-ering in the distance had been so terrifying...so devastating. It had been a lonely town where I had been abandoned, with shopkeepers too unkind to allow any free call services. Some were too creepy to have their shops visited.

The horror I had felt, the terror I had felt being scrutinized from the shadows, knowing that I was defenceless....that my husband did this to me...

The shock, disbelief, denial, extreme hurt, I had been a mess.

I had almost got kidnapped if it wasn't for a kind teacher who owned a local shelter home. She had taken pity on me while walking out of a shop with her father. She had seen my dishevelled, traumatized look, my bridal attire...the thick tears of pure devastation, shock and horror flowing down my cheeks, and instantly offered me support.

I couldn't go back to my family. I tried. I called my uncle, feeling too ashamed to call my parents, and was immediately told by him that I was no longer part of the family, that I would do my parents a favour by staying away and not causing them any more pain. I had done enough.

My uncle had warned me not to contact my parents. I had already been too much of a disappointment and heartache for them. It was best if I stayed away...it was best for the family reputation.

A missing daughter was better than an ashamed returnee.

My heart had broken once my uncle had abruptly ended my phone call, and I had realized that I had nowhere to go. The old teacher, Miss Hamna, took me in. Wiping my tears and introducing me to the other girls living in the shelter home, she had announced me as family. The reality of that announcement had crushed me.

My cousins, everyone, they would forget me now.

I had made one of the worst mistakes of my life.

My mum had been so right.

Anyhow, after one year, I had finally managed to become a monotone mess in the shelter home. I hardly smiled, hardly opened up...and the mourning and feeling of sheer regret were so real. The shelter home was horrible. It was shabby, smelly, unkempt and had its rooms stuffed with girls who got minimal food. It wasn't because Miss Hamna was unkind, but because this was all she could afford. She, herself, was hardly living above the poverty line.

Now, lying on my bed, with the usual tears flowing down my cheeks, and watching the leaky roof dripping with rainwater, I kept my arms folded. I could hardly sleep at night. The mosquito bites were a norm now. I no longer bothered with them.

"Sila, you awake?" Maryam, my roommate's voice whispered from the mattress beside mine. She was my closest friend in this house. Both of us had arrived with our wounds and heartaches. Both of us could silently understand each other. She was just a year younger than me.

"Yeah..."

"I met with Noreen from the stationary shop today. She said her brother is coming to our town in a few days."

"That is nice." Emotions were hardly felt by me anymore. I hardly cared about anything.

"She said her brother is some sort of sponsor, and that he might get us some jobs in another city." The information caught my ears.

"Really?" I didn't want to be given false hopes.

"Yes. She said that he might even be able to arrange cheap transport for us and some accommodation. He is looking for cheap labour. We will get to do some small jobs for a rather reputed company."

The whole offer was too salivating and dreamlike. Having no degrees with me, since I had left them all behind, I was hardly getting a job in this place. No one was willing to hire an inexperienced girl who lived with Miss Hamna. No one.

It had been shattering to witness my one terrible decision tear me apart at so many moments.

Moving out and starting with small jobs could be a much-needed breakthrough...

"Are you sure her brother can do all that for us?" I enquired, desperation echoing in my tone, as I turned to look at her.

"Positive. Noreen never fibs. "

Okay, so which city are we talking about?"

"Hill land. She said something about needing low-level staff for Kingston-a fairly renowned company."

Chapter 4

S ila

Loud sirens and horns echoed in the air. The opportunity for a new beginning...I shed a single bittersweet tear as Maryam tugged on my arm and pulled me through the crowd of travellers. We were all going to the Hill Land-a city of fine job opportunities.

The train station was overflowing with sellers, villagers and labourers looking to abroad the cheapest train and rush towards fulfilling their dreams. The sound of children crying, the loud mayhem, sellers and workers echoing in the air seemed too loud and profound. I was so overwhelmed.

The dry heat of the day was sinking in.

Flashes of my families, memories of loved ones hugging me, my cousins having tea with me, hurt my heart. I was all going to put it behind, as I was pulled towards the stuffy entrance of the green, local train. The conductor was almost hanging from the gateway.

"All abroad!"

"Here is our ticket!" Maryam announced happily, waving our tickets in her hands. Both of us having our small suitcases hanging from our shoulders.

"Get inside." The conductor rudely spoke, not bothering to check our tickets. This was how the peasant class travelled. A few village families were lining behind us. The smell of gravy and spices heavy in the air.

Upon placing a foot on the train, I momentarily looked behind to relish the feeling of all the joy this city had once brought me. I gazed at the familiar crowd, woman tugging their children around, vendors working their best to sell fruits to the travellers...this had been my home.

'Sila is the baby of our house. No one is ever supposed to hurt her.'

'Sila, we want the best for you. You are our everything.'

'Our baby Sila!'

As the glowing sun echoed in the air and my hold on the train's handle tightened, my emotions gripped me hard. I was going to miss my home so much. There had been so much pain and misery...my mistakes were always going to follow after me.

"Miss, stop blocking the entrance and get inside!" The order was curt.

Quickly snapping out of a strong sense of nostalgic despair and sorrow, I quickly nodded and stepped inside the train. The train's hallway was so overstuffed, hot, humid and dusty. Children were crying, making a fuss in their seats, mothers were sitting with huge cooking pots in their hands and their husbands were somewhere lost in the crowd. The train's windows were broken and dusty.

"Sila, here!" Maryam's giddy voice called out to me. She had chosen a two-sitter seat right next to the dusty window. Before her, two rural ladies were sitting with children sitting on their laps.

A tender and broken smile appeared on my face.

I had to accept that the hurt was going to stay, the regret was never going to leave me alone, yet this was my chance. After battling with extreme depression, this was an opportunity for fighting back.

There was sunlight was flooding the trains. I breathed in its sensation to strengthen myself and shook my head. There was hope. No matter what, a bright sun, a lit path, they always meant a chance. The pain of the past had been excruciating, yet I couldn't stay there anymore. I had to move on.

"Of course." I met Maryam's excited grin with a gentle and nervous nod.

Hurrying by her side while avoiding the crowd, I slumped down and allowed her to grab my arm in sheer excitement.

"This is it. Our chance to shine! Next stop, the land of opportunities!" She giddily rejoiced.

This was it.

A whole new chapter of my life was to begin.

Hill land-a a land of opportunities.

Upon reaching the city, Maryam and I had stepped out onto the railway station with awe in our gaze. The place was busy, crowded and seemed to differ from my simple home town. It was so much more diverse, populated and bright. The simple dresses had been replaced by office-like attires by many. Mostly everyone on our train had travelled here for jobs, opportunities and chances.

The buildings were so huge. We had been directly escorted to a taxi straight from the train station and were driven through the extravagant streets of the city. There was just so much culture here. With our faces almost plastered against the car windows, Maryam and I couldn't help but stare at the posh crowd-almost too rich and modern atmosphere on the streets.

Lamborghinis, Ferraris, Limousines, silver heavy beaks, neon light, everything was just a thickly rich echo of how to advance the city was. However, this rich part of the city wasn't meant for two broke girls. Soon, after being driven through the active site of the city, we were driven to its outskirts.

The outskirts was a silent and dry area. It was meant for those who wanted to find someplace in the rich city. Old small houses built close together, brown fields being used for keeping livestock, labour families stuffed together in one place, buildings, factories, shelters, were all found there.

My heart had shattered at the sight of some houses.

They reminded me of terrible thoughts. I had never belonged to this side. I had been dragged here by someone whose reality was this pain, and I had been a fool to let his scars pull me along. This wasn't my pain. It was his. Yet, foolishly, I had allowed him to shove his burden over my shoulders.

Feeling depressed again while staring at my fingers, I felt my heart sink along with the sunset in the distance and gulped in a broken sob as the blossoming feeling of reluctant eagerness swaying in my senses slowly morphed into a notion of despair and horror.

There was still so much struggle and endurance needed.

My heart broke completely as our taxi finally stopped before our destination; a dirty tall building with weed grown around it, shabby clothes hanging from so many of its balcony railings, black smoke blowing out of its windows and the sound of children emerging from behind its walls.

Maryam and I had to stay in one of its top floor rooms. Both of us had to share our rooms with two other female workers.

"Let's go." Maryam's excitement still was there, while I just felt quiet now. The image of a new chapter hoped by my mind had fooled me. The reality was so much different, painful. This place just seemed to fuel my sense of depression, regret and self-pity.

I had once lived on feathers...sheltered so fiercely and protected with a full will.

I had been so unfair to myself.

Soon, upon paying the taxi driver his fares and gathering our bags, Maryam and I began heading inside the building. Low crickets could be held cricketing in the air. The smell of oil was so fierce in this area. It was pretty difficult to breathe in this place.

"We will get used to it soon..." Maryam, noticing my disappointed silence, squeezed my hand in comfort with a warm look while working to balance her bag on her shoulder. I gave her a sad smile.

"We have to. We have no other choice."

"True." Her smile echoed with a sense of forlorn acceptance, while her grip tightened around my hand. She needed that. Her share of scars yearned for support, would have her cling onto even an ounce of kindness offered. She was scared of feeling lonely, and I had been damaged by opening up to someone. Our dynamics were opposing. Yet, together, we were working on healing our hurt.

We both had been betrayed by people...

We both were working on suppressing our devastating emotion s...

We both had been hurting for so long.

Inside, the building was brown carpeted and had a small reception desk placed right beside its entrance. There were hardly any people around, and the walls were covered by graffiti art. A rather reserved lady was sitting behind the reception desk. She was reading a magazine with a cup of tea in her right hand. A set of keys were hanging from a shabby wall, right behind her.

Walking straight up to her, I simply placed my bag on her desk and allowed Maryam to handle getting our names entered. She had been the one who had got all our residence details from Nora.

"We are here to stay in room 304." Maryam pressed her hands against the counter, sounding polite and confident.

"Course. Just take the staircase to the third floor. Our elevator collapsed a few days ago, the woman spoke in a curt tone, not even bothering to enter our names and get any information from us. "Also, if you see rats...just ignore. They don't do anything if you don't bother them."

Maryam and I simply nodded.

There was a time that just thinking of rats made me feel so skittish. Yet, ever since, I got to live at Miss Hamna's place, I was used to them. One couldn't afford to feel skittish or timid if they had to survive on these sides of the streets.

"Sila, I can't wait for us to be super rich," Maryam quietly spoke, lying on her mattress, with the moonlight falling on her face from the cracked window. We both had our mattress placed closer towards the door. Our room was small, furniture-less and had some random mess lying on the floor.

Our roommates, Zarina and Soha, were two teenagers who had also travelled here from small towns to work in the big city. They were quiet, different and couldn't speak the native language of this place. They had hardly spoken anything when Maryam and I stepped into the room.

Now it was deep into the night. And with Zarina and Soha snoring, Maryam and I were wide awake, just feeling the new city vibes.

"Me too..." A random tear rolled down from the corner of my eye, as I kept my arms folded while staring at the ceiling. My emotions were like this. They just spilt out; sometimes randomly, sometimes purposely.

"What will you do if you get a lot of money?" She turned to face me, pushing herself up with her elbow.

I momentarily lowered my gaze to heave a sigh and began looking at the ceiling again. "I don't know." My voice sounded tiny, tired and grieved. The pain would always threaten to spill over when I talked.

"Well, I will buy my own house. I go on a shopping spree. I will get us out of these horrible rooms..." She promised with so much hope, a dreamlike grin appearing on her face.

I met her gaze with a forced smile, reflecting my hurt.

She had a dream. I was just working to move on. I didn't have any plans, nothing...just needed some way to get back to normal.

"I just want to go back to my home." I couldn't help but blurt out. I never really spoke about this to anyone. I hated returning to that nightmarish regret, feelings...I hated accepting that how much I missed everything because saying it out loud just fuelled my emotions. I never wanted to talk about it.

"Sila, I-I-" Her excitement turned into anguish.

"It is getting late. We have to wake up early in the morning." I changed the topic, breathing hard to stop myself from crying and just breaking down. I was hardly keeping myself glued together.

"Okay." She sighed in defeat. "Just know that" her voice gained momentum again, 'I am with you. I know you don't like talking about your past. I know that you have been hurt by someone close to you. I understand your pain. You are the only friend I ever made in my life. And I know, together, we both can make this work. We need this."

Her confession brimmed my eyes.

Nodding mutely while feigning a yawn, I simply turned around and secretly pushed my face into the pillow. Once her snores began echoing in the air, I allowed myself to lowly spend the rest of the night crying into the warmth of my dirty pillow.

I was feeling so lonely.

Eliyas

Gazing out of the window of his apartment, Eliyas sipped on a warm cup of dry leaves tea. His apartment was everything he had hoped for; huge, modern and exquisite. He, Saud and his son had arrived here on a silver automobile and had immediately fallen in love with this place. It was the first time Nabeel had refused to sleep early at night. His son seemed happy.

Finally, his efforts were paying off.

He had worked hard to get here.

Chewing on bits of the leaves, he then looked at the neon lights shining below his window and half-smiled at the dreamy gleam of the city life. Everything was so tall, powerful and expensive here. It made him feel calm. He knew he had made the right choice of settling down in this place.

"Bro, I got someone to provide us with some guns and cheap heavy bikes in this place," Saud now walked into the apartment with a brown bag in his arms. He had gone out for midnight grocery shopping. "We can also visit this city's basement tomorrow.

Jamshed said that we need to keep ourselves updated. Your ex-admirer has already started using her father's resources to try and hunt you down. We need to be prepared," he announced, walking towards the kitchen.

"She isn't going to do anything big. Jasmine was too cautious about safeguarding her father's reputation. She will never let her search blow into a nationwide search." Eliyas simply shrugged, taking another sip of his tea. That girl didn't have the guts.

"Awesome. That girl was your best choice," Saud snickered in amusement, disappearing into the kitchen to place the grocery bag.

Eliyas lowered his gaze towards the cup.

She wasn't.

"Sila was." He simply spoke, memories flashing in his mind.

The day she had begged for him to stay...

She had been the easiest prey-too gullible, too innocent. Her gaze had been so soft. Jasmine, on the other hand, had been sharp, bratty and would try to act girly while acting super clingy and entitled, which was so annoying. She got on his nerves so many times, and he had to tolerate it with a charming smile to keep up the facade. Sometimes, he didn't even bother putting up that facade, and still, she would seem awestruck by his brooding ways. It was beyond desperate.

If he hadn't been too concerned about his son's upbringing, he would have stayed in his hometown just to witness the bratty princess's expression upon finding out how she had been conned. It would have been so worth it.

"True. True..." Saud nodded, chuckling again, now walking back into the living room.

"Wow...this place looks so gorgeous at night time. I am digging this city's vibes," he spoke conversationally, moving to step next to Eliyas.

"It does." Eliyas relaxed and put on a lazy smirk. his teacup almost empty.

"You were so right about choosing to settle down here, buddy." Saud squeezed his shoulder. "If your job works out for you, this can be our longtime home. I can even get married to some rich girl here and stop making rounds to the basement. We can put a hold on being on a run till Nabeel grows up."

"I know." Eliyas simply nodded.

This had been his plan.

He was glad that this city had turned out to be how he had imagined. It was a much-needed change from his old home.

"Good. Good." Saud now patted his back, yawning with a happy smile. "I am going to sleep now. Wake me up before you leave tomorrow. Jamshed has to take me to his shop tomorrow."

"Will do."

Soon, with silence echoing in the air again and the liveliness of the city peered in through the window, Eliyas pulled up a black couch before the scenery and slumped down on it, feeling the soothing sensation of the atmosphere pull him into a comfortable sleep.

These new city vibes were his new home.

Chapter 5

S ila

Smoky air, stale food and cheap yellow taxis were the tokens of my first day's start at the Hill land. Maryam and I had to wake up as soon as the sun was hinted at in the sky and were asked to get in a yellow taxi by a stoic factory man. He told us that this was going to be the routine for us labourers.

Cheap breakfast. Early morning starts. Late Night shifts.

The drive into the main city was quiet.

Maryam was super sleepy and kept her head resting against the glass of the car window. I sat in the middle of the backseat and kept absently staring at the view outside. The change from the dirty grounds to the rich city life was extremely spectacular. My nerves were playing in. And with the morning sun still to rise fully up in the sky, I was wondering how my first working day would go. So many fears, issues and imaginations.

The anxiety was so real.

After so long, I was going to do something new and try to move on from my past. This was my leap, and it had me so tangled.

Curling my fingers and feeling slightly better since last night's hit of extreme depression, I kept staring at the tall building before me with a thoughtful look and wondered when I would make some space for myself here.

Soon, our taxi stopped before an extremely tall and metallic building.

'Kingston Incorporation'

"Maryam, wake up!" I elbowed Maryam, with my eyes widen in awkwardness, as the gruff taxi driver simply pushed an empty tuna can towards us.

"Cash!"

"We are from the labourers' town. Our fares have been taken care of," Maryam groggily spoke, rubbing her eyes and sitting up straight.

"Okay." The man wasn't really happy with our response.

Quickly, before he chewed out more of his random mood swings, I pulled Maryam along and stepped out of the vehicle. The man immediately drove his taxi away. Slight shivers ran up my spine. That experience was oddly frightening and uncomfortable.

Momentarily looking around and wondering if anyone saw this, I grimaced to notice a few bystanders eyeing in our direction. This was a working city. People, here, were already on the roads to head towards their workplaces. The click of stilettos, office boots, etc, and the smell of coffee were so profound in the air.

"Let's go." Maryam grabbed my hand and pulled on it before I could get lost in the mayhem of the street noise.

"Course." Giving the tall building a once over, I gulped in lowly to calm my anxiety and started taking firm steps towards the building.

The Kingston building was a rich, corporate building with its different floors dedicated to several work areas; IT, Finance, Accounts, Marketing, HR, etc. They were so many departments on so many floors, with each floor too busy. Maryam and I didn't get to observe much before we were escorted by the ground floor's manager to the staff room.

Just one lady was sitting on a brown couch placed in the middle of the staff room. There were brooms, bowls, over-flowing cupboards, a sharp stench of chlorine, floor-cleaning liquid, soap, water buckets and random files stuffed inside this place. Also, there were only two couches and a table set here, which meant either this place had been miser when hiring low-level labourers, or that the staff members just didn't get time to sit.

The manager was a man in his forties and seemed to be of a foul temper. He stood before us with a stern stance, as he spewed out the instructions for us.

"You will report before 6 daily. You will join our staff's team and help clean, dust, take care of the files, sort them out, arrange the cupboards, take orders from the working staff here; serve them food, coffee and pass around any work files for them. Also, your shift will be flexible, but you will remain four hours behind after the work hours of this place. You guys will help make sure that the department you are appointed to is in spotless condition before the next morning. You will be paid a fixed amount on the first of each month, regardless of how many extra hours you work."

'Leave Sila alone. I don't want my baby to do any stressful work.

'Sila, don't wash the dishes. You will tire yourself. Let the helper lady handle it.'

'We don't let Sila do any work. She is our baby. We have her focus solely on her studies. Her future means so much to us.'

I had been pampered, loved and adored. I had been so heavily sheltered that I hadn't even been able to pick the first stroke of cruelty. There used to be so many helpers at my home, so many ladies working shifts, and I never really understand their efforts; the pain of working hard is a necessity of their lives. The efforts of low-level staff are often ignored and repaid in the form of minimum wages. No one really sees the hard work they do. No one bothers to hear their hurt.

Listening to all of my duties reminded me of how much I had to struggle to gain momentum. There was so much hard work and endurance needed from me. I had to go a long way before being able to stand on my feet. I had to work super hard, while losing myself completely in the process, to get somewhere in this city.

Tears brimmed my eyes, but I quickly suppressed them back with the determination to act strong. There was no time to break down here. Both Maryam and I obediently nodded with our hearts racing fast, feeling extremely overwhelmed.

"Okay, now Madam Zaina will give you girls your uniforms and your schedules. If you have any more questions, you can ask Madam Zaina." He gestured to the lady sitting with her back towards us. We mutely nodded again. He turned around and left.

Feeling a bit relieved to have him gone, Maryam and I turned to Madam Zaina with a hopeful look. The lady was sipping on a cup of tea. She placed it down and slowly turned towards us with a bored expression.

"I hope you like blue colour."

Huh?

"Your uniforms." She pointed in an obvious tone. "Go and get them from cupboard two."

"Oh"

Nodding, Maryam and I quickly rushed to a cupboard with 2 written on it and pulled it wide open. Inside, there were two transparent packets placed above some kitchen tools. The packets were stuffed with our uniforms and schedules.

Pulling out our stuff, both of us hurriedly opened the packets and shared a look.

Our uniforms were light blue and simple. Holding my uniform in my hand, I looked at Maryam, who seemed to be studying her share, and frowned. It was going to be awkward wearing a uniform in a place where everyone had the choice to wear their own formal attire. I felt embarrassed yet knew that I had to gulp in this emotion.

Heaving a sigh, I then looked at my schedule and tilted my head. My first shift was on the second floor-the HR department.

"Maryam, where is your first shift?" I quickly turned towards her.

"Finance department." She jokingly shuddered, making me give a soft smile.

"Sounds boring." I tried to ease our discomfort and hidden feeling of pain.

"I will meet you here in an hour." She announced.

"We will have tea together." Anything to take the sinking depression away.

Feeling strange and inferior in having to wear a uniform while others roamed around in their unusual attire, I tried to drink in my embarrassing tears and kept my gaze firmly on the floor, as I rushed to head towards the elevator. I felt ashamed, so low and tiny. I felt belittled and small.

Trying to not let depression engulf me, I kept telling myself that this is just how so many rich people started before earning bucks, that no one was watching me. The ground floor was full of white-col-lar workers, employees...everyone didn't have the time to stare at the low-level staff. I was just overthinking. My uniform was being looked at with disgust and a sense of superiority. I was just like everyone else. I was also to be respected.

Upon reaching the elevators, with my heart beat extremely frantic and nerves completely tangled, I saw an old man-some manager nod his head at me.

"Your floor?"

"Two," I spoke in a tiny voice, keeping my gaze on the floor, feeling inferior because of my attire. I shouldn't be.

"Yes, of course." He pressed the button.

Soon, an empty elevator moved to our floor. The man, instead of stepping inside, gestured me to go inside. Though hesitant and a bit fearful, I complied and was astounded to see him simply press the 2 button without stepping in. Wow!

This man had been waiting for the elevator much longer than me. He seemed some kind of a manager here, yet he had given me so much respect. I felt emotional.

"Thank you." My voice sounded so grateful. And soon, the elevator doors shut.

Inside, the privacy of the elevator made me feel comfortable, away from the scrutiny. I leaned against the silver mirror walls, breathing in to calm my anxiety. I could do this. The lights of the elevator were dull. There was a sweet fragrance echoing in its air and the small act of kindness by that old man had somehow given me a little boost. Some people had to work hard in life. So many rich and influential people started from here...

I had to let go of my depression and pain if I needed to get somewhere.

No more breaking at every single point.

I had made mistakes, and it was time to start doing something about that.

Soon, with a little prep talk, I straightened up as the elevator finally stopped before a crowded floor. There were so many cubicles on this floor, men working on computers, helpers moving around while carrying trays, files. I felt momentary shy before working up the courage to walk out of the elevator. I had to work here.

Awkwardly stepping out while not having a clue what to do here, I stiffened as I saw a janitor now walk towards me with a tray in his hands.

"Finally! Here, go and serve this coffee cup to our boss sitting in room 2. Also, after that, go and bring a cloth. You are to dust and mop for today." He bombarded me with tasks. The noise of the floor was too much for anyone to focus on me. Also, the floor was too overflowing that it made me feel comfortably invisible. Perfect.

Nodding, glad to know I had something to start with, I grabbed the tray with confidence and breathed in. Finding room 2 didn't seem a problem here. Behind the cubicles, there were so many rooms that were numbered.

Carefully manoeuvring through the cubicles, I managed to reach a dark-brown door with a golded plate plastered on its upper part. On the golden plate, it was carved: room two.

Splendid!

Prepping myself to seem professional and formal, I knocked on the door and slowly pushed it open. My heart was beating so fast. I always felt awkward meeting new people. It was because of my anxiety and mental issues. There was always this sense of fear in me.

Carefully balancing the tray in my hands, I walked inside the room and saw a man standing behind a desk that had been placed before the wall opposite me. There were bookshelves pressed against the right and left walls. A wall-length window right behind the desk, covering half of the wall.

My heart...it had suddenly turned so frantic. A terrible feeling sense, a state of denial of knowing something but not wanting to face it...my face was turning pale, blanched, hands shaking, as I halted into an abrupt stop, only to have my terrible fears confirmed as the man looked up, his eyes narrowing in surprise.

"Sila, he wears rings and is mostly found on the streets. The air guns you hear at night...it is him and his friends. He is not a good man, my dear.'

'Please...I know I don't have a good reputation on these streets.'

'Sila, run away with me.'

'I am sorry...'

Everything started blurring. Suddenly, I felt so back in my mind, so disconnected. My head had unconsciously shaking no...while I began spontaneously backtracking. I could hear my frantic heartbeat loud in my ears, the abrupt disconnection with the world. Tears brimmed in until my senses snapped in at the sound of a mug smashing against the floor; the coffee now creating a pool around me. My panic attack had been triggered.

An audience gathered around, but I didn't care as terrible terror, despair and a sheer feeling of excruciating devastation hit me hard. He was here. The man who had ruined me was here. My nightmare, my torture...I had moved all the way to face him again.

The anxiety, the panic...suddenly, I couldn't breathe. Hands grabbed me, but I didn't care. I couldn't breathe!

"Madam!" Many shouted, yet my nightmare stayed at his spot, behind his desk.

"I-I can't-t breathe!" The hysteria was catching up with me. "I can't breathe!" A sense of dizziness was hitting me hard, and before I knew it, my consciousness began drifting away. The shock, the terror, my soul had been moved so badly.

There were just empty, panicked noised around me, as I swiftly lost myself into a state of unconsciousness...as my heart hid from my nightmare.

Chapter 6

S ila

Waking up on a foreign white bed, I had simply sat up straight and cupped my face, sobbing into the palms of my hands...crying my heart out. He was here! With my money, he had been having the time of his life. He had been earning positions, posts! That dreadful night, it forever haunted me. He was here. My nightmare, my ruination...the man responsible for it all was here, and I just didn't know what to do. Questions were rising...how did he even get here?! How! What was he even doing here! This city life was supposed to be MY escape, yet he was here taking that away from me too. I felt so devastated...so trapped.

My mother had been so right. I should have never spared this man even a glimpse. He was going to crush me whenever I tried getting up, moving on. At all opportunities, he was going to ruin me. I had moved to the big city for opportunities, and he had appeared to ruin that too. He felt like some parasite that wouldn't leave me alone.

He wasn't going to leave me alone!

Suddenly, I was feeling so trapped, so suffocated.

I had been brought to the nurse's office. There was no one in my room, and the door had been left ajar. There were people still super busy outside. The world seemed to be busy as usual outside, yet inside the white office, I sat on the bed completely trapped....what was I going to do....my heart was mourning.

Eliyas...another wave of hysteria and pain hit me so bad. That man was just so horrible. He was just so terrible, and he was here again, in my life. What was I going to do? Facing him again terrified me. I gripped onto the bed with steely strength, staring at the white marble floor with the thought of what I was going to do now...just what was I going to do. My one chance of moving forward, making a place already felt out of my grip.

I just didn't know how to hold on anymore.

"Sila!" A frantic Maryam now rushed into the nurse's room, looking extremely concerned for me.

Seeing her pushed me into another wave of heartbroken hysteria, feeling so wronged, so used and tiny. Crying, I allowed her to just pull me into a hug and try my heart out. After suppressing this for so long, after trying to avoid it all...all the pain, all the humiliation of being a wronged bride, it had finally spilt out, and I couldn't control it anymore. After such a long time, I cried my heart out on Maryam's shoulder, I cried over my mistreatment...just how hard it had been...how badly my heart had been hurting all this time.

I was truly heartbroken.

Like a small girl yearning for a single hug, I held onto Maryam. I needed it. I needed this so much. I had been needing this for a long time. I just wanted to go back home. I just wanted to stop feeling miserable. Despite trying to feign strength, I was the heartbroken wife who got thrown on the streets by her husband. I was broken.

"There, there..." She consoled me, hugging my back. "What happened?"

"T-The m-man who l-looted me is here. The m-man who c-conned me... became the reason b-behind me l-landing at H-Hamna's place is here." I couldn't help but finally cry it out. There was no point in hiding this pain anymore. He was here! There was no point in moving on anymore. I had to accept that he had destroyed my happiness.

"What the heck! Do you want to report this to the police? Who is that man...how did he manage to con you?"

"Apparently, he is some boss of the HR department. He used to roam in my streets...and h-he fooled me. I have no proof to convict him." Tears burst out again, and I pushed my face deeper into her shoulder. The memories, that night, had just refreshed in my mind. I was hating it.

I was hating it so much.

I was so crushed.

"Okay...just wait here. I will get you a glass of water. You are going to make yourself ill." She rushed to grab a glass of water from the nurse's table.

Sniffing, I nodded while looking at the ground absently...my eyes were so puffy, emotions just so exhausted. I was just so tired.

Outside, I could hear the nurse finally head towards this room. I was on the ground floor. With the help of the ajar floor, I could hear the nurse talking to someone.

"The poor girl just fainted. She was assigned to the second floor..."

The person said something in return, causing the nurse to speak again.

"Nah. She is a newbie here. I think the hiring team made a mistake. The workload is so much here. I don't think she will be able to manage working here for so long. Oh! Wait!"

"What?"

"I forgot my gloves in the chem room. I will just go and grab them." The nurse rushed away. Both Maryam and I shared a devastating look. I felt ashamed.

This incident might cost me my job.

I might have to go back to Madam Hamna's shelter house again-that horrible place.

"Here," Maryam now sat beside me, handing me a cup full of water. "Drink it in three sips."

"Of course."

Moment of silence echoed in the air, both of us thinking our own depressing thoughts until Maryam spoke again.

"Sila, I think you should not let that man get to you again." She willed with a determined expression, making me look at her; soul feeling completely vulnerable.

"He destroyed your happiness once, crushed you. Don't let him do that again. He is not worth you ruining your chances to move on and get better things. This is an opportunity for us. We worked hard to get here, travelled miles. We got this chance, and no rotten heart is going to take that away from us again.

You deserve to be happy, Sila. Forget about the past. We need this to move on. Soon, in a couple of months, with enough money, we can find another job...and this man...he can be a slave here for as long as he wants. He will no longer be a part of your life, and you will have managed to get back all you lost because of him. Don't let that man push you down again, take away that chance from you.

I will be by your side. Together, we can do this. Just pretend he is not here. Pretend he isn't working here. This place is huge. You can easily avoid him."

She was right.

Listening to her words, breathing in and focusing on my feet, I knew that her words were wise. They made sense. I couldn't let Eliyas get to me again. The past happened, so be it. I couldn't let that destroy me anymore. I couldn't let go of this opportunity because of him. I couldn't let him take away more from me. He had already done enough. My family deserved my strength. I had to be brave for them.

"You are right." I nodded, taking a sip of water to calm my senses, to steel my heart. I kept looking forward as I spoke, "You are so darn right."

"You need to rest now." She then gave me a tender smile.

"Do you think the admin will allow me to go back to our flat right now? I need it to think for a little, just to deal with the shock..." I needed to regroup again. If I was going to make this work, I needed some time to work on my nerves.

"Yes of course. The admin knows you are not feeling well today, so it will be perfectly alright to go and get some rest. I will inform our bosses. This is just your first day. They will definitely not fire you because of one small mishap. They will try you for a couple of days. Go...I will call our taxi again. Just make sure you get a lot of sleep." She hopped off the bed.

I gave her a nod.

Maryam had turned out to be such an endearing friend, support.

The ride back home was full of so many thoughts. I kept staring out of the taxi window, remembering so many moments. My walk to the college with my cousins, our family fun nights...we were such a team.

My family was my biggest fan. They all loved me, adored me, had my cousins and me studying at the best institution. Never were my dreams and wants to be rebuked. I used to get every luxury that I wanted. I had support, love...and I had thrown it all away...for what? A street criminal? I was fortunate, yet I broke my family's trust. The words that were spoken to me by my uncle, when I had wanted to return back, had crushed me.

Moments of laughing with my cousins, having my cheeks pulled with adoration, the cooing, the family love, they made me shed lonely tears. I missed it all so much. I missed being that carefree, naive girl who adored exciting books and loved to daydreams...who was the biggest fan of fairytales, cliches...

While leaping for the stars, I had forgotten about the diamonds of the ground.

I was so fortunate.

There was no point in being ungrateful of being hidden in the shadows. I had wanted to have my own voice, not realizing that I had so many already listening to my unspoken words. There was no point in rebellion when I had been so sweetly kept on cotton dreams and adored by strong shields. I had been such a fool. The epiphany had hit me hard. It made me sniffle back tears,

Upon reaching the flats, seeing how the beauty of the city morphed into the sadness of poverty, hardships and work, I looked out of the window with a mind that willed that I didn't want to stay in this neighbourhood anymore. It was time I realized that as much as Eliyas had wronged me...I was of as much fault as him. I had broken my family's trust, insulted their love for just some sweet words-a sheer stranger.

I had betrayed my family.

Getting out of the taxi, I then watched with low emotions, as the taxi spun away from me. It felt like I had been pushed back so hard, shoved so harshly away by the world. Under the open sky, I was alone. Even with echoes of laughter, people around, I was so alone, so hurt and just so miserable. I had been hurting for such a long time. Today, my shoulders were just slumped.

It was about time I worked to move forward, forgave myself and did something. Eliyas...it was about time I stopped letting his betrayal and his rough ways control me. So what if I was still tied to him. I couldn't let that man destroy me anymore. Giving him any relevance in my life would be foolish. I had to let the past stay in the past. There was no use crying over spilt milk anymore.

What's done is done..

I had to stop feeling irritated and frustrated by the fact that I had been roped into marriage by a con artist. Taking slow steps towards my flat, seeing dirt and smoke echo in my surrounding, I knew that I couldn't stay in this place anymore. One of my roommates was inside the flat, eating some dried bread, as I stepped in. She looked up at me and then went back to feasting her treats. Unlike before, her mannerism didn't bother me today. This was my reality, and I had to accept it. No more self-wallowing.

Throwing my bag roughly on my mattress, I then made myself a cup of dry tea, wanting to relax my nerves, and moved to sit before the window. Outside, the sinking sun made me close my eyes. allow one lonesome tear to fall. I folded my eyes and breathed in.

That night, that entire experience, it had been such a lesson. I had learned, I had lost....and I had really seen life from a different angle.

Taking a sip of the warm tea, I breathed in again and just stared. The smiles of my family, the charming smirk of Eliyas...all the beauty and deception in my life, I had witnessed the sinking sun. I had to wait for dusk. It was about time I reached for it, instead of hiding in the nights.

As the sun sank into the ground, I finished my cup of tea and looked up with determination.

I could be strong.

I was going to be strong.

Chapter 7

S ila

Some people have to work hard for morsels, while some are destined for wealth. I had learned that my smiles weren't meant to be offered. I had to work for them, fight for them and endure that many around me did enjoy smiles offered free of cost.

The throw of money, the ease...it wasn't until mud water was thrown over my uniform by a speeding Ferrari that I learned that dignity, respect and wealth were expensive deals. I had lost them all while searching for love. My pride in my charm, that may be thought of being loved, they were my doom. Yet, today was another day.

Down, low yet willing myself to act strong, the cold stone weighed on my heart, as I entered my workplace again, the noise inside me screaming a lonely cry, wishing to unleash...yet that noise was my peace. There was nothing I could do. I had to scream to the hollows of the darkness residing inside me and pretend that I was being listened to.

Maryam had an early shift in the day. I had been given some relaxation because of my health, but it was time to get serious. My workload, today, included no visits to the HR department. Stepping inside the building, I heaved a sigh. The shame of my uniform...it screamed that Eliyas had won. And I was just here to show that I had accepted that and was willing to move on.

Dreams of marriage...to be loved...to be adored...

The reality of emotions is that sometimes they scare their selves. Sometimes, our dreams are so big, and we are so eagerly looking forward to living out our fantasies, that we break our hearts. I did it. I broke my heart by craving a fantasy that was just full of lies.

Bitter and weighed by the status showcased in my uniform, I lowered my head towards the ground and began preparing myself for a brand new day. The whispers, silence...they were all biting with the anxiety that, perhaps, my yesterday's show-of-weakness was being gossiped about. However, to blank it out was my solace of the day.

Just black it all out...

Memories did try to resurface. The haunting sensation when he had abandoned me...that shock...that pain...it almost did bring tears to my eyes. Yet, I would will myself not to go there. No more. My future depended on my will and the counselling of my soul that it was going to be okay.

Eliyas...I was optimistic about the fact that I could ignore and avoid him here. Just a few more mute encounters, and then his chapter would close, and Maryam and I would manage to shift towards enjoying the real perks of city life. The frustration that he was already enjoying the city life while I had to work for it was immense...but I just had to gulp in that bitterness if I needed to move on.

The anger, the budding frustration and pain...I had to gulp it all down if I needed to stand up.

With my uniform shaming my dignity, I began taking firm steps towards the staff room. The busy life of the business workers was as per the routine. Nothing had shifted or even turned, while my whole world had greyed with newfound caution. I had to stay silent to the scream inside of me.

Suppressing the voice would be my solace.

Blanking my emotions into a monotone, I headed into the staff room and felt my stance tighten at the sight of Madam Zaina sitting on the brown couch and chewing on some tea leaves. Her gaze reached mine in a rather patronizing manner.

"You feeling better today?" There was no warmth, just an experienced person judging a newbie for apparently slacking off at work.

"Yeah..." I had to breathe, shifting my gaze towards the floor in awkwardness.

My anxiety had been acting up. Talking, just being put in the spotlight, felt overwhelming. I wanted to just stay low and remain camouflaged in the shadows. The shameful weight of my attire would weigh heavy when anyone would focus upon me.

"Okay." Madam Zaina just kept staring with a rather distasteful expression, chewing on her tea leaves with exaggerated bites.

Trying to control the tremors budding inside me, I began picking on my sleeves, nodded to own self in reassurance and then moved to grab a bucket, mop and cloth from the cupboard.

Placing the cloth on my shoulder, I began carrying the mop and bucket outside and felt a strange weight rest on my heart. The envy of respect...in a place, where anyone could easily snap at me or treat me with disrespect, Eliyas was being treated as a boss. It seemed wrong, frustrating...

A person who had hurt me so much was living his dreams. It made my pain feel insignificant and unimportant-like the agony was just too inferior. The complexes and insecurities, which I had developed, felt damaging. I even considered my hurt inferior and too unimportant to be looked after.

I avoided meeting Madam Zaina's judgemental gaze, not letting it bite into my forced sense of dignity, and kept my head held up high as I moved out of the staff room. A rather pained chuckle almost got spilt out as I wondered how she would react if she knew that my husband was a manager here; one of her bosses. Yet, my thought disgusted me. The man who had abandoned me...I needed no favours from him.

Eliyas would mock me for even holding such a thought.

My shame would never let to heal from such an embarrassment.

My dignity had been so badly crushed, that I had started thinking as a desperate people-pleaser. I never used to be like that. Once, I was annoyed by those who tried to butter up others. I guess I had been too naive, too sheltered to understand the concept of desperation and need.

Sighing, I finally stepped out of the staffroom, quietly shutting the door behind me. The pierce burn of a judgemental gaze still had me slightly shaking.

Outside, the floor was busy and crowded. This was my solace: the crowd. It was easy to turn invisible in the storm of people.

I kept my gaze away from the elevators, on my far-right side, not wanting any unwanted encounters and reunions, and began heading towards the cubicles that were just a path-a row- away from me.

Feeling awkward, I kept my gaze lowered, as men talked past while talking on their Bluetooth. The general shame of belonging to the low-scale staff bit me. Breathing in, I then began heading towards the cubicles while making my way through the crowd.

The cubicles had men working energetically on computers. There were cleaning and helping staff rushing around these people and making sure that they were served. Tea was being served around. Nimko, biscuits...files would be caught before being dropped. I had to momentarily pause at the boundary of the cubicles just to stare at the view before me.

The office chaos...the work...thankfully, my shift was only limited to this floor today. It gave me peace to that out of seven days, there were a few where my heart wouldn't have to be constantly fighting an unresolved battle.

Rushing frantically past me, one worker was almost about to drop a tray full of tea on me.

"Move!" Harshly snapping at me, yet not being loud enough to be heard over the noise of the floor, the man rushed to serve the people on the floor.

"Go clean Madam Sheila's office; room 9." Another one then walked towards me from the right. He seemed the head of the clean duties on this floor.

Nodding immediately, I finally willed myself to officially begin with my duties. I had to walk through the cubicles to reach the office rooms. Walking behind rows, separated by low walls, I could hear men laughing and generally having a good office time. The place, which was career-boosting for many, was just my rough experience.

I kept my head lowered, as I moved behind the chairs...avoiding them. My breath hitched when one man abruptly pushed his chair back and got up. He was almost about to bump into me. He didn't even bother apologizing, as he made his way to the cubicle on his right.

With my back now facing the cubicle, I momentarily stood listening to him apologize to some employee whom he had nearly bumped into while reaching his friend's cubicle, and I began to take strong steps towards the offices. I had to block it all out if I wanted things to finally work in my favour.

Steeling myself, I finally reached room no: 9 and knocked on it. All the doors of this building were the same. Yesterday's events re-forced into my mind, yet I just had to ignore the salt of familiarity and numb my emotions.

The bravest strongest are, sometimes, the ones that can suppress their emotions.

"Come in..." The order was firm.

Nodding, I straightened myself up in a professional manner and pushed my way into the room. Inside, a woman in her thirties was sitting behind a desk that was placed before the wall opposite the entrance. She was talking to someone on a Bluetooth while typing on her laptop. Her office had small square-sized windows. She seemed extremely organized. There was just a cupboard placed in her room...on the left side of her desk, pressed against the wall.

An empty cup of tea had been placed next to her laptop, with small droplets of tea accidentally spilt around the coaster and maligning the crystal shine of the white desk. I knew what I had to do.

The woman briefly met my gaze, and then went back to doing her work. She was talking in fluent English with someone on the phone.

My vocab, spoken and grasp of English were not as polished as hers. The touch of fast city life...this place had no room for authenticity and being true to the roots. The demands of the international markets were being met here. I was a simple girl. I had raised with the morals to be proud of my roots and language.

"Madam.." Adopting respectful and professional conduct, I immediately moved to pick the empty cup of tea from her table, leaving my bucket and mop behind. Quickly cleaning her desk with my cloth, I winched as an irritated scowl appeared on her face as my hand accidentally brushed against the edge of her laptop. I was standing on the opposite side of the desk.

Sweating slightly and trying not to shake, I quickly completed my work, mumbled a quick apology while staring straight at the teacup that I had now picked up, and turned around to subtly rush out of the office.

Mistakes, blunders...disappointing anyone on this job, they worried me. I didn't want to lose this job. My yesterday's drama had already been enough. I wanted to move on from this chapter in my life. The sudden cling of desperation hit me hard.

I was so easily replaceable here.

Eliyas's position guaranteed less hard work and more money, while I was worrying one disappointing anyone here. All of these people had more relevance in this building than me. I needed to fight for my place here.

Clenching my fists tightly, I was about to grab my bucket and mop when Madam Sheila called out to me. "I need salad and ice tea in about fifteen minutes. Also, make sure that the serving is for two people." Her voice sounded curt and strict.

A simple change in tone can crush a person's dignity.

Turning around, I folded my hands and obediently nodded. "Yes, Madam. Of course." I almost sounded too desperate to earn the approval of this woman.

With an edge depicting in her gaze, she simply went back to working on the laptop. She had switched languages to speak to me. This was the liberal elitist class that used language as a way to show power. It depicted their complexes and insecurity. While trying to copy others, they had lost pride in their own identity. It was pitiful.

With the teacup held steadily in my hands, I began walking out again while feeling determined to get started with my new task. Once outside, I was just about to close the door, when I heard Madam Sheila laughing in an oddly cold manner into her Bluetooth.

"The managers are heading out for lunch today. After our lunch, we will have a meeting about the contract. We will probably sign the deal today."

The contrast between two different realities...I was seeing the glitter from the other side while knowing that it did glow. One blunder and I had fallen into such a devastating pit.

Love, feelings...the fantasy coaxed in my mind, they were responsible for pushing into this mess. Closing the door, I listened to the laughs echoing from the cubicles behind me and promised; promised to never again feel vulnerable emotions. To be weakened by my feelings had been a big loss. The walls around me had thickened...were so high up now, and never again was I to let anyone reach me, get to me again.

The foolish notion of senseless love...I hated it so much. It was stupid thinking from the heart instead of the mind. Life needed practically, and I was going to be exactly that; practical, logical and strong. No man was ever going to make a fool of me again.

The tears in my wounds were going to become steel solid.
Never again would I let anyone become my weakness.

Chapter 8

S It was calm before the storm. Weeks set into place and a routine had formed. Every morning, Maryam and I would set out for work, and every night, we would return too tired to bond with our roommates. Soha and Zarina; their cultural iciness and different personality were becoming manageable. We had learned to work around each other.

The walls had set.

Maryam had been so right about this place being too huge for more accidental encounters with Eliyas. During my shifts at the HR department, I would simply keep myself hidden in between the cubicles and make sure that my back faced Eliyas's office door at all times.

I would work extra hard and appear to look super busy, so no one would consider me for taking tea or food to Eliyas's room. He hardly walked out of his office, with workers often being the ones to visit him. I dared no peeks into his office and ignored the whispers of gossips of the floor that were both admiring and fearing their department's manager. Also, I would work my best to move out of the HR department, as soon as possible.

There was a sense of aloofness, a constant zoned-out mood, as I would work on cleaning the second floor. Memories of the night ...that haunting night...the way, I had pleaded and begged, his sad apology, they were a constant battle to numb against while working on the second floor.

Eliyas had turned even more gorgeous with age. It was an excruciating discovery that broke me every day. The bad-boyish street biker was a white-collar boss. The day I saw him here, he had been standing so tall and powerful, looking so confident. and that change had bitten me. It had bitten me so ruthlessly. I had lost my voice while my abuser's had just turned more powerful. His charm has just increased tenfolds, while mine was insulted by everyone.

I had to watch him celebrate the trophy of ruining me.

Soon, my moments of bliss ended and the storm that had been threatening behind the calm finally blew in.

"Sila, there has been water spilt in Sir Eliya's office. Go and mop it!" The in-charge of this floor's cleaning staff called out to me. I was one of the rare workers of this place that worked super hard and never said no. My first impression had been so horrible, yet I had managed to work my way above it.

"S-Sir..." Picking up an empty teacup from one of the cubicle desks, my hands almost shock as I turned out. The hyperventilation was real. I-I was strong. I had to be strong.

The head-incharge hadn't waited for my refusal, as he had then moved on to overlook what the others were doing. I trembled.

"Bring me some Nimko and pastries after that." The man, who was sitting a few steps next to me and working on his computer, spoke without even looking away from the computer. I nodded in a breathless manner, a gulp of dread stuck in my throat.

I wanted to talk to Maryam. The prep talk she would give me...it would be helpful in numbing my emotions again. One surprise order and I had been hit by an explosive feel of hysteria and panic. I needed to regroup and put on my facade again. Yet, I knew that there was a need to be urgent and quick. The only show of hesitance, and the head-in charge won't think before screaming at me before the crowd. I couldn't let that happen here, especially on this floor. Being screamed at, with Eliyas being in hearing proximity, would crush me.

Blanking out...I had to blank it all out.

This was just a one-time thing. I would just keep my gaze on the floor and quickly do my work. No exchanges, no interactions...not facing him would help in pretending that he wasn't there. The terror that man-induced inside of me, the trembles, I had to suppress it all.

Slowly, I picked up my bucket, mop and flung my cleaning cloth over my shoulder. Emotions had been ruined. Still, the moments of that horrendous betrayal, felt like souvenirs as I began taking steps towards my oppressor's room.

The memory of that love...they stared deep for a second, and the loss of my youth hit me. I had wasted my smiles and love over a con man. The air had turned gloomy. The atmosphere around had turned into a blur, with each step daunting a heartbeat that yelled caution and resistance.

Files flew around, men kept laughing and shouting over my head, workers trespassed my path, yet everything had vaporized. I was looking at the ground with a tunnel view, fists clenched and heartbeat intense.

Calm...Calm...I had to focus on this sensation, this emotion...

Calm...blank it out.

Memories of that wedding day hit, and I squeezed my eyes shut...I would never let anyone walk away from me again. I would never let anyone turn their back towards me. I would never be that girl again.

Breathing in, I finally made it towards the dreaded door, momentarily focusing on the chaos behind me, and then knocked on the door.

A worker...my status...he had stolen it.

He was my boss.

The remittances of my dignity had crushed under my feet. I was accepting my defeat.

"Come on." The tone was cold and busy.

You are a good girl, I can tell. You belong to a good family, and I don't want to discomfort you in any way. Just give me a chance..."

Breathing in, I walked into the room.

There he stood by the window, with his back turned towards me. He was talking to someone on the phone. his Rolex silver watch flexing under the gleam of the sun. He was randomly tugging on his pristine white shirt's collar, as he stood speaking to someone on the phone in fluent English and staring at the glorious city view. His leather shoes were sparkling with a rich gleam, and he had his hair pushed back by gel in a professional manner. His stance, everything had improved.

There was water spilt a few steps behind him, next to his desk.

I had to clean his mess.

The image grabbed my entire calm and solid strength.

I shook...

I should have seen the signs. A street biker...I should have known that I deserved more respect. I should have seen the burns that he was leaving behind. On my heart. My reality. I had dreamt a picture. I shouldn't have let him see my yearning for affection as a weakness.

Now he stood...so tall, strong and successful, while I had allowed the demons to ruin me. So many opportunities, chances...and I had allowed this man to use them as a step for his own success. The comparison between us would definitely make people side with him now. I would be considered lucky to have once gained his attention. The tables had completely turned.

Feeling the gulp of emotions and the overflowing burst of agony hit me again, I lowered my gaze towards the ground, taking slow steps towards his mess. I was on the edge of breaking down. Seeing his again was something I had underrated. Encounters with him were always going to haunt me, destroy me. The shakiness was real.

Trembling, while forcing myself to not think and just focus on the spilt water, I clenched my fists to control my tears and bent down on the floor. There, next to the dirt, on the level of his feet, I began wiping the spilt water.

The humiliation, the degradation...

Tears were threatening to fall, but I sat down on my folded legs and began mopping the floor. I was trying to focus on the feeling budding inside my heart, to just stare strictly at the floor and not hear his deep voice gave orders in an authoritative tone. I had married this man. It was a grieving pain.

Wiping, I lowered my head further towards the ground, as I felt him turn around. My heartbeat had turned erratic. I didn't want him to see me, notice or recognize me. I didn't want him to witness my humiliation. His feet drew near, until they stopped a few steps before me, right next to his desk. He was still talking on the phone, with a trail of spilt water leading up to him.

I moved to clean that, making sure not to look up, and gasped as he stepped on the water trail. The move seemed assertive. Spontaneously looking up, my eyes widened at the sight of him giving me an amused smile while still talking on the phone. His gaze was fixated on me, as he turned around and leaned against his desk, folding one arm. It seemed as if his gaze had been fixated on me for a long time.

The dangerous malice gleam in his eyes, his sadistic enjoyment at the sight of me moping the floor before him, there was a hidden smirk of arrogance. He was in no mood to acknowledge me. It appalled me.

How did I never see how dangerous this guy was?

How did I never notice the dark and sinister vibes? There were so clear, so crisp.

The way he was staring down at me, watching my humiliation...

He then stepped aside, in a show of giving me space to clean the trail of water. I blanched. He turned his head to look out of the window again, as I watched with a purely tortured and heartbroken expression. He was ruthless.

The man who had once promised to love me, to take care of me... the man who had begged me to marry him, he had been so callously watching me from heights. There was mercy, no remorse. This was the person for whom I had betrayed my family. The notorious biker boy. I had rebelled against a disgusting criminal.

Subconsciously, I had thought that he might hold a bit of remorse. Even that night, he had tried to keep his words a bit gentle. There was a tender apology gleaming in his eyes, yet now that facade was completely over. These were his true colours.

He seemed so smug at the sight of my destruction. My tears welled up again, and I lowered my face towards the ground and began hesitantly clearing his mess. I was near the level of his feet, as he didn't inch away. He wanted me to stay at that level. He didn't move an inch, as my mops moved to wipe water droplets an inch away from his feet.

My nerves got completely messed up.

The collapse of my stance was real.

Emotions grabbed me completely. I was feeling so embarrassed, degraded and low. He was purposely putting me in my place. I had no idea why he was doing this to me. What did I ever do to this man? He had taken my money, left me...and now he was again chosen to crush my self-esteem beneath his leather shoes. I had no idea why he was being this brutal...

Did he see me as a pathetic and desperate girl who had so easily abandoned her family for him? Had my respect in his eyes diminished the moment I had chosen to ran away with him? Good girl...this society had labels. My mother always told me that even bad boys respect the girls who respect their own selves?

Eliyas had once called me a good girl.

Did he no longer see me as a respectful person?

It was strange how some men toy with girls, support their boldness and encourage their rebellion. They make fools out of the girls, and when the naive ones fall for their lies, they tend to label them because only the good girls are to be respected. Not fooled, hopeless in love ones. People are quick to put labels on the unsuccessful ones...the weak ones.

Hurting others should never be an option,

I hadn't been desperate. I had actually trusted someone. He had promised me so much, and I had fallen for it. Now he no more saw me as a challenge, and he had moved on. He had treated me like trash, and I was the one who got to be labelled as the sad pathetic girl who had lost the right to be respected. Eliyas...he had simply tricked me using the most obvious lies. People saw me as a fool.

Trusting people, not judging stereotypes and listening to stories, had turned me into a fool.

This society was meant for sharp players.

Shakily, I cleaned the floor, feeling a hiccup of cries gulp in my throats, as my pitiful state hurt me more. I couldn't believe what was happening to me again. I was being humiliated by this man again.

Eliyas was beyond cruel.

I had destroyed myself for this ugly-hearted man.

Whimpering and trying not to burst into a fit of hysteria, as the agony was brimming my heart again, I got up...feeling dishevelled by the haunting sensation resting in my heart. Fear was making me shake. This man...he was terrifying. His brutality scared me.

I kept my gaze strictly on the floor, breathing hard to keep my tears in.

Not here...Not here!

The tremors were real. My prep talk wasn't working much. With legs wobbly, I had just turned around and was about to head towards the door when the pristine tone of Eliyas called out to me again.

"Thank you. Please do ask Saleem to get me a cup of coffee. Also, I want my lunch here at about fifteen. Make sure it is picked from Palsey and served on time. I have a meeting at 2 o'clock. Tell Saleem to make sure that I am not to be disturbed at that time. Also, I need my files to be rearranged by tomorrow."

The blissful calm behind the storm...

I had reached the storm. I was a prey finally caught in the trap. The predator had dug in its claws and was finally in for the fight.

Dread and horror were reflecting on my face, as I numbly nodded.

"Of course." The words were tight and controlled.

This was the start.

Chapter 9

Sila

I cried on Maryam's shoulder. One humiliation, one blow... and I cried for hours on the woman's shoulder who understood my pain. That night in our room had been so nauseously suffocating. We had to hide our devastated cries while our roommates slept with dirty pillows that were covering their heads. Both Maryam and I had decided to sit and just cry into our own palms.

It was those exhausting moments when hearts decided to finally overflow.

The sad shade of the moonlight had fallen on the floor of our room and engulfed us in a sorrowful manner. For hours, we had just cried silently, in a broken manner. We were two women bonded by our pain. Maryam understood it.

The faint fumes of the dirty smell of our motel aggravated our pain. The depressing situation reminded us of our losses, and we cried...until the rays of the poetic moonlight started vaporizing. It was then the calm came and shoulders felt light.

"We can do this," Maryam spoke, both of us staring out the window. There were just poverty and hard work outside. We were prisoners of our choices.

"I know." I felt...empty yet, strangely, better.

Sometimes, we just need someone to cry with us.

The smell of Gulam-ka-Arq (rose water) was strong in the air. Our roommates loved spraying that water in the room. They loved greasy food, using natural herbs and crushing their own spices. There were from villages where a manual and simple way of life was preferred. Their dialect reminded me of home. There used to be helpers at my home that loved spraying rose water everywhere. I used to smile at their antics. Now...there was just sad nostalgia.

"You made a mistake. See him as a wrong choice and just ignore him. He is not worth your tears. Monsters like him never are. Let him live this life with a silver smile. This is just temporary. Everyone dies. He can't escape that."

"I-I know. B-But it is tough," I sighed, tone heavily, as I looked down at my fidgeting fingers. "That moment when he had so arrogantly stood before me and watched me sitting on the ground, wiping his mess...it was humiliating. He did so much. And I h-hate how he was gloating his victory. He was flaunting his power while treating me as just a speck under his feet."

"He was rubbing it in my face how he had made a complete fool out of me, and there was nothing I could do. That helpless, low and inferior feeling, I hate it so much. I hate how I allowed that monster to marry me. H-He is so arrogant, and I acted like such a desperate girl for him. He must see me as the most naive prey. I can't believe how much of a fool I made out of myself."

"Slam that loser with a divorce! Immediately!" Maryam fumed, getting caught up in the intensity of my words.

My rant halted immediately.

Divorce...

My chances of heading back home...breaking ties...there would be permanence in that. How would I ever be able to earn my way back if I lost the status that I had rebelled for? People are merciless. The destruction of my future...it would gain another title. I didn't want to snap into that version of reality. I didn't want to face it. My dreams, everything...I didn't want to face that hardcore reality of how badly damaged that fantasy was now.

A path of destruction...ruination...all roses had wilted away...

I didn't want to face the real picture of Eliyas's cruelty. There was still an edge of denial, some grip, I didn't want to space the heart-wrenching bit of reality locked away in my heart.

Trembling, I shook my head. "I-I c-can't. I don't w-want to face t-that chapter yet. The damage he has done. I don't w-want to face it yet."

"I understand." Pity seeped into her tone, and she patted my hand.

There was misery in my stance. I was panicking. The chapter pricked...it was pushing me into a state of hysteria and anxiety. The panic attack blossoming inside...I didn't want to deal with it.

My gaze began swaying around, breath hitching as I tried my best to push all dark thoughts away, and a warm sense of calm grabbed my palm, as Maryam held my hand.

"Hush...relax. It is okay. I will get you some green tea. It is fine. Just ignore that man now. It is fine. Just breathe in. You are giving that man way too much relevance in your life. Relax....see him as a sinful being and just ignore him. He is from the streets. Many men from the streets often belong to ill-mannered backgrounds and have no morals. You are a good person. Be patient. Patience is always rewarding."

"True..." I tried breathing in to keep my calm.

There were trembles. I had severely underestimated Eliyas. My limbs were still trembling with a sense of fear, yet soon...I knew that I needed to move on. Strength, ignoring that man, would be the key. I had to show patience. There was no point crumbling at the sight of that monster. My family deserved my strength.

Taking deep breaths were making me feel cold since I was winning against my panic attack and managing to suppress it down.

Calm...blank it out...lock it all out again.

Calm...

A cycle started, a circle formed.

Soon, the game began.

Eliyas began asking for me to clean his mess, room and manage his files. Every time I would enter his office, making sure to ignore him and keep my gaze diverted, he would so arrogantly order me around while working on his laptop. I was a mere worker.

At moments, he would spill tea or drinks when I would be almost done with my work or mix up the files' order. He seemed so nonchalant and casual about his careless antics, that in the beginning, I was seeing his mistakes as honest antics made because of an occupied mind, yet soon, a constant pattern was forming. There was consciousness in his clumsiness. I couldn't believe it. For a grown man to be this immature...it was so frustrating. And he was playing it as if all of his mistakes were accidents.

Emotional abuse...

He was choosing to emotionally wound me while leaving no substance for me to fight against. He making me clean his office. It was my job. I had no grounds to complain about that. Also, I was just a low-grade staff. My complaints would be snubbed immediately. The boss could make me do whatever he wanted.

I would already be feeling overworked because of my shifts, and he was adding more to many duties. Sometimes, I didn't know if I wanted to cry in despair or pull on my hair. I would do my best to simply ignore and complete my work...yet I was edging towards losing control. Eliyas was just so obnoxious. This was my money that he had leeched upon. My wealth! It seemed so unfair how arrogantly he was enjoying wealth that was mine!

It was my luxury! My status!

The street bikers were the notorious punk boys of our town. I had decided to give one of those rowdy brats a chance. I had decided to give him a chance. And now...it was like being constantly crushed under his feet for the choices I had made. I was constantly being reminded of how much of a fool I was; his naive victim. I hated him so much. The audacity...

He would work so nonchalantly on his laptop, sometimes purposely step on my mop as I would be wiping it across the floor. He would push over my water bucket, do so much and act as if I was just one of the many workers for him. It was beyond degrading.

However, soon, my emotion of showing calm and ignoring Eliyas relapsed.

Now sitting on my legs a few steps before Eliyas' desk and wiping the floor again, since he had complained in a distracted about that I had left the edges, I was almost done with my work when a glass filled with water came tumbling down on the floor. Horrified, I looked up at him in shock and devastation.

Oh no...

"I apologize." He was giving me a rather guilty and apologetic look, yet there was a hint of mischief in his gaze. His hands were now folded on his laptop's keyboard in a sophisticated manner.

Tears pricked my eyes. My limbs were aching. I had been working since morning. I was so tired, hungry and exhausted, and this man just wasn't having mercy on me. This all was a game for him.

I-I had enough!

I stood up tall, watching, as he raised an eyebrow at my sudden change of aura and then leaned back in his armchair while placing his elbows on each side of his armchair and folding his hands in the air. He was seeing this as a sadistic form of entertainment.

"How dare you! How dare you do this to me!" I began taking fumed steps towards him, crushing the glass pieces under my shoes. My temper had finally snapped. No more! I wouldn't take this anymore!

"Do you think this is a joke? Do you think I am not picking on what you are doing here! These accidents...I may have been a huge fool before, but not anymore. I know the real you. You are heartless! After ruining me, you still have the guts to keep on doing this to me! You are disgusting! I regret sparing you even a minute of my life! I hate you! I hate you so much! Just wait! I will make you pay! I will make you pay for all that you have done to me!" My temper was soaring so high up, as I gripped the edge of the desk.

He was looking at me with a rather amused and mocked-scared expression as if I was some insane woman who was blowing at him for no apparent reason. His reaction was making it seem as if I was the crazy one, and it was aggravating me more.

Frustrated by reaction, I grabbed an ink pot that was placed on his desk, right near the edge, unscrewed its lid and threw the liquid at him. This was my outburst, a pure show of acting on my emotions. It was the adrenaline rush and the loss of control that had me act so barbarically. All my pent-up hurt and frustration had finally decided to flow out, and I was working on a complete rush of instincts.

"What the heck! Are you insane!" The moment he yelled and got up, as the coloured liquid soiled his clothes, was when I finally snapped out of my anger-induced rushed. I hadn't meant to do that.

"Oh no..." I had gasped in horror, backing away, feeling shocked by my own actions. Yet, this was just the start.

With a clenched jaw, Eliyas wiped the ink dripping from his chin and got up. Moving away from his seat and rounding his desk, he came to stand inches away from me and harshly glared down at me.

"Just what do you think you're doing?" He sneered, eyes almost bulging out, as the nerve in his forehead visibly throbbed. He was angry. Aggressive angry. His fists were curled in a show of temper. There was ink dripping down his clothed arms, spilt on his legs.

I was standing, back curled in reflex, frozen, hiding my tremors and a feeling of fear, staring up at him with a terrified look.

"I-I am putting you in your place." I decided to fight back, trying to keep my feeling of fear hidden. I had to hold my place and be strong. I couldn't let him get away with this. I had to put up a brave front while I worked to flee from this room. Thankfully, the walls of this place were solid thick and there was chaos outside, or else, this fight would definitely have attracted a crowd. I just hope no one decided to step in, right now. I was already on the verge of getting fired. This man...I was going to lose my job because of him.

"You are a low-grade worker here. You should know your place," he spoke, gritting his teeth and towering over me to intimidate me with his height.

Slap!

I couldn't control myself. I had panicked. The moment he had looked down at me with a rather frightening and harsh glare, my strength had collapsed. My heartbeat was racing so fast, and his words just angered me more, so I snapped.

One harsh and powerful strike against his cheek.

His head only tilted a bit to the right, and before I knew it...I was slapped right back. Though his hit was just skin-deep and hardly too strong. I should have felt humiliated. I should have felt so degraded by the fact that a man had just hit me. My cheek was throbbing red with the impact. However, instead of all the hurt, all I was feeling was an insane level of adrenaline rush and mad fury.

With a clenched jaw, feeling totally disgusted by this beast, I furiously raised my hand to slap him again. Yet this time, he grabbed my hand, as it neared his face, and raised his other hand towards my face. I momentarily closed my eyes on instincts, yet a soft caress of fingers against my right cheek made me snap open my eyes. I looked at Eliyas, feeling surprised and completely caught off guard.

His furious expressions had morphed into an intense look. There was a gentle notion, as he stared deep into my eyes, treating my cheek as the most delicate skin. His jaw had unclenched, as he seemed to be in some sort of a stance...a notion of hidden awe, tenderness.

I quickly snatched my hand that was still in his grip and moved back, scowling in disgust. Wordless, I turned around and stormed out of the room.

I needed a break.

Eliyas

The moonlight sparkled down in a poetic manner.

The city view was gorgeous from the apartment's window. The moonlight was making the neon-lit buildings shimmer and dazzle in a mesmerizing way. Eliyas had turned off the lights, dragged the living-room couch right before the window and was staring out in a rather lazy manner. He was lying sprawled on the couch, one hand hanging from the armrest and the other caressing a red rose in his hand.

Wilting roses...he enjoyed deep poetry and nature.

After punching his heart out today, he had finally relaxed into his tame moods.

The delicacy of the flowers...tonight, they seemed even more beautiful and deep. Looking down at the rose, Eliyas twirled its petals, observing its layers and delicacy, and lowly chuckled as they reminded him of what had happened in his office today. A half-smile appeared on his face.

Her angered look...it was oddly endearing and amusing.

A furious rose.

Lost in his thoughts and observations of the flower, he didn't even jolt as the apartment door opened and Saud stepped in.

"Nabeel missed you today," Saud spoke, a strong stench of grease and oil accompanying him.

"I tried to wake him up when you were gone. He is a stubborn sleeper." Eliyas still not looking away from the rose, crushing its petals in his hands.

"Just like you." Saud chuckled.

"I am going to visit the basement tomorrow. Don has been messaging since morning about this deal. He wants to know if I am willing to get some cash for him. He thinks I owe him for old time sake."

"My wife is here in this town. I am being a good man for her." A nasty smirk appeared on Eliyas's face, as he clenched the flower and looked back at his friend. Saud was grabbing some mints from their coffee table. He looked up at Eliyas with a mischievous grin.

"But-" Eliyas's smirk turned even more sinister and malicious, "she won't mind me making a few bucks. And I am sure she would love to meet Don."

"Darn! So much for laying low here. I almost feel pity for your Mrs. That girl made the worst mistake of her life when she decided to love you," Saud laughed, shaking his head. "Finally, let's cash in. Bring her around. I will go with you, guys, to the basement. We can hire a babysitter for tomorrow."

"Deal."

Chapter 10

Sila

The choices one makes in lonely solitude are often the wrong ones. My desperation, insecurities and the serene sensation that someone wanted me had clouded my heart. My wants had been my greatest downfall.

My self-esteem was in ruins.

Now, after the red glaze of temper had cooled down, anxiety hit me hard. I had messed up. My job...I didn't want to lose it. Not because of him. Not because of a man who once had my heart. Maryam had been right. I couldn't give up on this city life. And with my credentials right now, no one was going to hire me. People from the city don't hire street rats. I had no credentials, could offer no background checks. I would be dumped back to Madam Hamna's if I failed on these lands. I didn't want that. At all. I couldn't go back to that stage of my misery.

Anxious, trembling, I stood beside Maryam in one corner of the staff room and kept biting on my thumbnail. She was looking at me with deep pity, worry and sympathy. Both of us had arrived early to our shift today. Last night, we had spent dreading the morning, and now my hysteria was finally catching up with me.

"He will get me fired today. He will make sure that I don't get hired again!" I was panicking, rocketing back and fro on my heels. It was the start of an anxiety attack. Heart palpitations, the feeling of doom...the fidgeting...I was losing control.

"We can talk to him. I can tell him that what happened yesterday was a just mistake..." Maryam suggested. She was feeling my pain, worrying for me.

"No...No..." I frantically shook my head, grabbing her arm in desperation.

Apologizing to him would be so degrading! He didn't deserve it. This was all his fault. I couldn't apologize to him for doing this to me. I couldn't give him the upper hand again. It would crush me if I had to take back all that I had said to him. I couldn't. I couldn't lower my shoulders in defeat before that beast. To see him look smug and give a victory smile would be my doom.

He deserved to be thrown in jail!

"Okay, then why don't you just go and talk to him? Tell him that you are tired of his antics and don't want to keep letting the past drag on. Tell him, that you have moved on and no longer care about the lost wealth or his betrayal, also, that is high time that both of you develop a professional attitude. If he sees that you are no longer a threat, he will stop bothering you."

"B-But I don't want to let that go." My voice cracked with so much hurt and frustration. "I don't want him to simply get away with my ruination. I want him to suffer. I hate him so much! I want him to pay! I want him to regret hurting me!" I fumed, gaze moving towards the ground, feeling hot tears brim my eyes.

"Sila," Maryam coaxed me to look up, her tone tired and realistic, as she sighed. "I know. But, sometimes, in life, we don't get closures or apologies. There is no point in waiting for words when that wait is just holding us back. Just let him be him. He is ruining his own life by living on stolen gains. Tell him that you are done with the past. You need this. You need to stop letting him get in the way of your strength." She rested one palm on my shoulder.

The impending sense of panic and anxiety had me shaking. The haunting sensation of muttering soft words for him made me feel scared. I didn't want to face that beast again. He had hit me yesterday. I couldn't give in first. It would be just another blow to self-esteem. I couldn't raise the white flag in this fight. He had to apologise to me!

'O-Okay." I nodded, hesitant. I had no other choice.

I was at a spot in my life where I couldn't afford stiffness. I needed to see marrying Eliyas as a mistake in my life and just move on. I couldn't confront him. I couldn't challenge him. I had to assure him that I wasn't a threat. I couldn't fight the battle he was willing to wager on.

I had nothing to offer in this war.

He had stolen my strength, shield and just left me as a ruined survivor.

I couldn't offer anything.

The agony in my heart was huge, and the realization and repetitions of epiphanies that had called out my defeat were crushing. I had to give in first. I had tried to ignore, close my eyes to sheer reality and now, it was time to officially announce my surrender. I couldn't challenge a man that was too dark, too dangerous, sinister and had no limits. Eliyas's didn't have a heart. I did. That is why I could never win this game.

Emotions only crush soft hearts.

Matured enough to understand life, I knew what I had to do. Soon, the morning work-clock struck, and Maryam and I began with our duties. It would be later in the day when I would have to go and tend the HR department. I was dreading that shift.

A kind old man pressed the lift button for me, and I felt so filled with gratitude. It was sweet that some people still chose to help others despite the status difference. However, once I stepped inside the life, I felt the feeling of dread and anxiety catching on.

It was time to deal with some consequences.

Upon reaching the HR department, my heartbeat grew wild with anxiety. The floor, as usual, was filled with white-collar men working inside cubicles, staring at their computer screens. Cups of tea were being served around.

Once I entered the arena, I was immediately handed a pile of files.

"Organize them and then give them to Sir Junaid."

"O-okay," I spoke, breathing hard and anxious.

I was feeling tiny.

Trying not to tremble, since my nerves were dreading my choices, I began to move towards a table that was pressed against a wall that was situated behind the cubicles, between the office doors.

I felt shaky, as I manoeuvred my way through the cubicles, being completely invisible for the white-collar men, and then moved towards the tables. There was always a sense of disrespect in this place. Men here, they didn't respect me as a lady. I was just a low-wage worker for them. Orders would be harshly and carelessly shouted in my direction. The man who should have fought for my respect was busy degrading me.

I was caught under a shoe that didn't mind stepping over my dignity.

However, despite been given a task, my mind was fixated on just one thought; I had to talk to Eliyas. I had to save my job. The fear of losing my chances was immense. I didn't want to lose this opportunity.

Dreading the thought that he would humiliate me more, I began doing more tasks, until a moment of rest was finally offered to me. I now had the time to do some damage control.

Placing a tray full of empty teacups on the serving table, I then breathed to gather enough courage to walk into Eliyas's office room. I hadn't been called to the admin office yet, so there was a high chance that he still had to complain about me.

I knew one call from him, and I would be replaced. He was the important worker here. I was just one of the many low-wagers. I would simply be screamed at and kicked to the curb. I needed to wave the white flag since he suffered no losses if he didn't. I was the only loser here.

Gulping, I finally mustered up enough courage and headed towards Eliyas's office room. I was waiting for someone to stop me, call me out...distract me. I wanted to be stopped, yet no one did, and the fear grew.

With my heartbeat racing wild and skin paled by anxiety, I hesitantly knocked on the door.

This was it!

My nerves were completely tangled, and sweat had gathered on my forehead.

How was I going to start the conversation?

What if I triggered him and worsened the situation?

I was petrified of the consequences.

"Come in." His cold voice increased the panic in my heart.

Eeeeeeps!!!

Hesitantly pushing open the door, I stiffened at the sight of him straight at me. He started smiling as he saw it was me. Somehow, his smile scared me more. He seemed in some sort of mood like he was up to something.

"E-Eliyas...." I reluctantly began, stepping inside and closing the door behind me, my eyes swaying in all directions to avoid looking at him, as I fidgeted anxiously. My head had lowered slightly. I didn't know what to say, how to say the words that crushed my dignity.

"Umm...my sweetest wife. Just the woman I wanted to see...Come, I want to take you out today." He stood up, grabbing his coat that was hanging from the backside of his chair.

His words chilled me.

What the heck was he saying?

"Excuse me?" I was so confused, taking a step back.

He didn't mind my words and then moved around his desk to walk towards me. His smile was boyish, charming....had a motive.

"I-I am not going anywhere with you." I looked up at him, fear instilling, heartbeat racing with dread.

What was he up to?

"You are not?" He playfully raised one eyebrow and then came to stand before me. The huge smile was still on his face. He was terrifying me.

"N-No...I-I came here to talk-"

Abruptly, he grabbed the back of my neck harshly with one hand, causing me to yelp out loud, as my breath hitched, and I gave him a trembling look.

What on earth was he doing!

Staring down at me, he squeezed my neck slightly, pulling me forward, smile no longer there, as he met my gaze with a malicious gleam in his eyes. His jaw was clenched now, mood serious and stern.

"You are coming with me today. Or else, you and your little friend, here, will enjoy the consequences. I don't like being disrespected. And what you did yesterday...I think you need to be put in your place. Don't you agree?" A mean smirk appeared on his face. I started trembling in fear.

Oh, no...

He, Maryam...no...no...no...

I couldn't let him hurt Maryam. I couldn't let him destroy her too.

Panic and fear hit me hard. He couldn't do this to us. He couldn't do this!

"I will report you! I will tell the admin what you are doing to me!" I threatened, trying to get him to let go of my neck, my voice is high pitched and panicky. Immense terror was rocking my nerves.

What was he going to do!

"And they will believe that the manager of a firm is bothering with one of the lower-workers here?" He raised one eyebrow in a patronizing manner. "Seems to me that this is a case of a poor woman looking to climb up the ladder." A malice-filled smirk appeared on his face.

I knew he was right.

I knew that no one would believe me.

I was trapped.

"I-" I didn't know what to say.

"However, if you do go on this little trip with me today, I assure you that no complaint will be registered from my side. Not in the coming days at least." Bullseyes. He had me right where he wanted.

I didn't know what to say or do...

Completely trapped, I nodded in defeat. "Okay."

Down the building, outside to his parked car, I felt like one of his prisoners that were following their captive. My heart was sinking so low. This horrible person...why on earth did I ever give him a chance!

I was such a massive fool!

I was so desperate and naive!

Street bikers, notorious for being rowdy and dangerous...all red signs were there.

Why on earth did I not trust my parents!

My heartbeat was racing so fast. It felt like a sense of impending doom, as I sat in his car. A notion of Deja Vu hit me so hard. Fear and anxiety increased tenfolds. The last time, he had decided to drive me around, he had dumped me in the middle of nowhere.

Was he going to do the same?

He was probably, and I couldn't retaliate because he would hurt Maryam too. I couldn't let Maryam become the victim of my mistakes. Eliyas had been my choice. Not Maryam's. I had to pay for trusting this man. Not her. I just hoped that once dumped, I would find my way back home.

The feeling of terror and anxiety almost had me breathless.

"Please don't dump me at any place." I pled, as he sat down on the driver seat and grabbed the gear.

"You will be back at work tomorrow." With no other words offered, he simply started the car and began driving.

The torture had begun.

In the shabbiest corners of the city, down some old corners and inside a grey building, I was lead to some restaurant that screamed corruption, crookery and thieves. Inside the restaurant, men were sitting on dirty yarn-mats, placed on the floors, some listening to the local news being played on dirty radios, some counting coins and passing around cash. The smell of smoke, gun-powder and stench was so strong in the air.

I had been led to one of the mats.

Now, sitting on my folded legs, with my fist placed firmly on my knees, I was staring strictly towards the dirty ground. Beside me, Eliyas was sitting with one leg lying straight and the other leg curled up. He had one elbow resting on the knee of his curled up the leg and one arm placed behind my back, on the ground.

There was a constant smirk on his smile, as he was enjoying the scene before him.

A crude man, with a huge moustache, was sitting before us and scaring the wits out of me.

"I say 10 grands would be enough price for her," Don was discussing my cost. "She seems too fragile, too delicate. What a gem!" He chuckled sinisterly. I was staring strictly at the ground, not even daring to look up. My heart was racing so fast, tears threatening to fall.

I was so terrified.

Eliyas was an extremely dangerous person.

This shabby restaurant, made me realize that I had indeed messed with the wrong side of the streets. I had got myself mixed up with extremely dangerous people. Criminals, gangs, mafia, this side of the streets were best kept away from, and I had directly ventured into it.

Street biker...no...I had seriously underestimated Eliyas. He was a man not to be trifled with. Human traffickers, dealers, he had ties with all. I had been so foolish to dare deal with Eliyas.

Trembling, little whimpers escaped, as Don praised me more. Eliyas was sitting so relaxed and comfortable beside me. He was enjoying how another man was terrorizing the woman he married. The fears would increase...

Would Eliyas sell me?

He could! The anxiety was real! He could dump me here and cash me in!

"She is so sweet. Look how she is trembling..." Don then mocked me in a playful yet patronizing manner, chuckling slightly.

"Little doe," he then addressed me scaring me out of my wits, "you wouldn't mind if-"

"Shut up now, Don. Stop messing with her." Eliyas then laughed beside me, sitting up straight and stretching his arms up, as he yawned. "We are going home now. I will talk to you about our deal tomorrow." Eliyas grabbed my hand. I didn't pull away, because I wanted to get out of this place as soon as possible.

"Sure. Take care of Nabe-"

"Don't." The harshness in Eliyas's tone chilled me. He sounded so strict and firm. "Saud will come here later. He wanted to come with me, but he got busy."

"Of course." Don sounded nervous.

With his large hand wrapped around my wrist, Eliyas began leading me out of the place. Many men sitting, snickered as my trembling form walked by them. Completely ignoring them, I kept looking down and stumbling my way out of the building. It was too overwhelming, too scary till I was led out to the open streets. I was barely holding onto the feeling of control, forcing myself to not collapse.

However, once outside, my waterworks finally started. Immediately tugging my hand out of Eliyas's grip, I pushed my face into my palms and began crying. I had felt so terrified, so scared. When Don had been suggesting my price, the dread had been so immense.

It was such a horrible experience.

There was a white street light shining above my head, with the streets around it completely darkened. I was feeling so very alone. This experience...it had completely crushed my sanity, traumatized me. No girl should ever experience what I just did.

The fear of being sold was so dreadful.

"Stop crying..." Strong hands tried to pull my hands away from my face, yet I immediately jumped back, glaring at the man who had done this to me.

"I hate you! I hate you so much!" Words blurted out, yet there was caution and fear. I needed to be careful here, so Eliyas would take me back to that horrible place.

He would sell me.

"I don't care. I want you to calm down!" He stressed, thundering to stand before me.

"No-"

"Do you want to go back inside?" He scolded, threatening me, his gaze harsh.

"No, please..." I began begging, looking at him with so much fear and anxiety.

"Then calm down..." he ordered, wiping the tears dripping down my face roughly with the back of his right hand.

"O-Okay," I breathed in, trying to gain control again.

I needed to stay calm. I needed him to drive me back.

"Come on." Grabbing my wrist again, he began leading me towards this car.

It was quiet, as he led me to his car and had me sit inside.

The trauma...I had just experienced what was going to stay with me forever.

Eliyas was a dangerous criminal. I had been a fool to try and confront him. I had been such a fool to underestimate him. Exhausted by my own emotions, I stayed mute as Eliyas drove me back to Kingston Inc. I was feeling dishevelled, so totally lost.

The torture had been so draining.

Silent, under the roars of the moonlight, I struggled with emotions and the haunting sensation that I was trapped completely. My ankles felt chained. One tug and I would be pushed into a world of torture and trauma. There was so much dread. I had been declared expensive, and Eliyas loved money.

It could be a backup plan.

I-I needed to leave.

Chapter 11

S ila

I was at that depreciating spot again. The sense of Deja Vu was intense, as Eliyas dropped me in front of Kingston Inc and then screeched off, driving into the darkness of the empty streets. The air felt chilled and lonesome.

Abandoned...dumped...

I watched as his car disappeared around the corner, the horn blaring loud in the air, and soon turned into a distant sound. It was quiet again. The street turned light and audible.

Standing on the steps of the Kingston Inc, I rubbed my shoulders in an awkward, drained and depressed manner and just stared at the corner behind which Eliyas' car had zoomed off. My shoulders were slumped. There was a sense of numbness, shock...

The shops and stores around me were still open. There were people busy with their businesses. No one was truly paying attention to the broken girl who had been ruthlessly dumped onto the streets. This was the city life. No one had time.

Wounded by mental scars, I then sighed and looked up at the changing clouds...my thoughts so far away, a rather sombre, serious and sad expression on my face. I felt quiet, defeated.

I was at that spot again. I was that girl again who had been ruthlessly dumped by a man that was supposed to be her shield. It was a reminder of the promises he had broken, how I had to fight to forget that phase, and yet here, I was again...alone on the streets.

There was a dream that I had once yearned with so much passion; to fall in love, to be wanted so purely and strongly by someone that made me forget my insecurities. Yet, all love ever did was remind me of my insecurities, entrap me in the brutal side of the streets.

To love, to lose...to hate him so much that one day I would manage to love my scars...

I had read about the victims of toxic relations; girls become prey to criminals. Stories of women destroyed by their husbands always made me wonder about the choices. The choice to love and beak. I was breaking.

Personalities change...we give our naivety, our laughs to people who don't even deserve it. I was the love of his life until he decided that I was unlovable, that my love could be turned into liquid cash.

The noise and glamour of the city life sizzled around me, and I watched the shining mood with a deep sense of despair. I was on that road again. The lonely road...the terrifying road. It felt like a huge storm had blown my way, and I was just standing...alone, so devastatingly alone.

I missed my home, the time when I was so sweetly wrapped in the dose of naivety and shelter. I knew nothing about the world, and that ignorance was bliss. Now, someone declared as a shield by our society, had screeched away, leaving me so unprotected and fragile on the streets.

My husband would sell me.

The traumatic experience, the shock of being a battered and lonely victim...I would become a victim of my choices. Mine; because crooks hunt and prey upon their victims. I was the one who had made this game easy for them. The disgusting praise of Don, and how Eliyas had actually made me sit before that man was so disgusting and heartwrenching. I was actually hating my own strength for not being able to do anything about it.

Shoulders slumped, with deep mourning and defeated feeling rushing through my veins, I sighed audibly until a hand grabbed my shoulder from behind.

"Let's go home." The voice was quiet, serious and understanding. Maryam.

IIn my moments of pure loneliness, defeat and heartbreak, she was here. When I was feeling so empty...missing my home, I had been offered someone who was seemed as light in the midst of darkness.

"What are you still doing here?" I asked. tears still echoing in my voice, yet I was just feeling so grateful that she had shown up. My dishevelled stance and wild pain felt growing tame in her presence.

"I heard some odd rumours, and I knew that I had to stay back...for you."

Momentarily, I just stared at her. My tears had reached the brim of my eyes, yet I was feeling, sniffing back my pain to deny reality. The odd sensation of numbness soon cracked, and I hugged her tight, placing my head on her shoulder and just crying my heart out.

There was no need for words.

Maryam had heard my pain.

"It will be alright." She patted my back in a tender and sympathetic manner.

Clouds thundered in the atmosphere and lightning roared in the air.

"It will be alright."

I couldn't go to the police. I couldn't file a case against Eliyas because I had no proof that he was terrorizing me. I was just a helper at Kingston Inc. People would see me as a clout chaser. Courts in this town worked for the rich. No one would support my battle. I would be deemed as a gold digger and punished. My image would be ruined. I couldn't afford to humiliate my family more than I had already had.

The trap had been set.

Resign; that was the only way.

It felt like I had been pushed back into a place where I had to coincide with the reality that I had failed. I couldn't go back home. The day I had chosen Eliyas over my loved one had been it. I couldn't keep on chasing after the past. I had to accept reality, and the reality was that I had destroyed myself, made myself available for the horrors of the streets.

A shielded life...and I had messed up.

There was so much, so much regret. Tears rolled down my cheeks, as I stared out of my building room's window and sniffed back the tears. Today, only I was awake. Maryam was sleeping. She still had a fighting chance. Yet, I had to give up. I had to give up the opportunity to aim for a bigger chance and heal because I had to...hide.

Depression...

Sometimes, the whole world turns to appear in just black and white colours.

I was trapped in my own brain, hearing my brain scream yet no words escaping out. The terror of being sold, the way Don had been so disgusting towards me, was so traumatizing. I had felt so weak, so vulnerable and trapped. Tears brimmed in my eyes again.

Memories were torturous now.

How could I have put myself in such a situation? How could I have allowed a man to destroy me like this? That emotion...that feeling...it was one of the worst emotions to feel. And now, I just had to feel it and move on. Go back; that thought terrified me. I didn't want to go back. I didn't want to go back to Hamna's. I was so scared. To live that chapter and become a volunteer prisoner again, I couldn't go back.

I couldn't go back!

I needed to stay here!

Yet, I couldn't, and the thought was crushing me.

Eliyas had taken so much from me. I had nothing more to offer, but still, he wasn't content. My dignity, pride...wealth...I had sacrificed it all for love. He still wanted more...so much more.

Staring at the night sky, I pressed my palms against my eyes and just cried. There was a sense of doom and defeat.

Tonight, I was celebrating the gloomy fall of dreams.

Tonight, I was finally accepting my ruination.

Eliyas

Placing one hand on the frame of the window sill, Eliyas stared down at the lit city view. There were heavy bikers roaring down the roads and a lively crowd rushing across the streets.

The city was fully awake tonight.

Yet, there was still a sense of silence. Staring down, Eliyas could only hear the silence of his apartment and the dark tinge of his place. He was standing in the shades, while the city glowed with a glorious sensation.

"You look upset..." Saud walked up to him with a blazing hot cup of coffee.

"Tired." Eliyas corrected, still staring down, watching as one racer biker roomed through a crowd. The city brats loved to show off their expensive toys. The shrieks and awes of admirers resonanted in the air.

"So, Don has been spamming my mobile with calls...why aren't you picking up his phone? Beside the other deal, he also loved the girl. He wants her. She would be a good investment." Saud handed him the coffee cup.

Breathing in the scent of the coffee beans, Eliyas slumped down on the sofa placed a few steps behind him and relaxed back into its leather. "He is not offering a reasonable price."

Saud came to sit on the arm of the sofa. "How much is he offering?'"

"Fifty."

"Are you serious? That is some good cash."

"Maybe." The tone was chipped and bored.

It was business...pure business, and each investment required a thought.

However, this investment required both the need to think and be in control. Tonight, he had felt an addictive emotion of control and power, yet at the same time, there was a slip in that feeling. A monster had ignited. He felt furious, mad...his temper had rocketed.

Don, Sila...

Visiting the basement had left him in a foul mood. After spending hours, thrashing a punching bag, he was back in his place, yet his emotions were raging. The fury was real. His tense muscles made him feel irritated. It made him want to drag Sila back and further terrorize her with the threats of her being sold. Seeing her whimper, tremble and scar would bring him a gratifying sense of calm, and he hated how his control was needing that emotion.

"Make up your mind before that girl gets the guts to hide. I won't be surprised if she is already on her way out of the city. You should have just left her at the basement. We could have decided about the price later."

"She doesn't have any place to go. We still have time. Beside, I think my wife deserves to have her husband bargain a better price for her." The malicious smirk was back on Eliyas's face, yet this time, it also held bitterness.

"Fifty is more than enough. That foolish woman would have ended at being sold for ten if she wasn't your wife. Also, I think Don wants to marry her. He was complaining that his wife and son have started to nag and whine. He needs someone young and quiet. Sila will do. Divorce her, and then sell her. Easy cash. Nabeel's day care center is charging legs and hands. We need the cash."

"I am going to visit Nabeel's day care centre soon. I need to know if how my son is fully enjoying their services. He has been sleeping more, smiling less." Eliyas shiftly changed the topic, a sudden feeling of protectiveness and firmness gripping him hard. He had started dropping Nabeel off at one of the finest day care centre of the city. He needed to make sure that his son was okay with their services.

"They adore him. They play a lot of games with him, which probably tires him out. Also, Nabeel missed you. Just take a day off and spend some time with him. I am travelling to the fields in a couple of days. You can take a day off when I come back. We can take Nabeel to the basement, show off some automobiles. The trooper would love that."

"Okay."

"And, Eliyas..." Saud now got up from the sofa's arm.

"Your knuckles are bruised. Go easy on yourself. I know today is the day. I miss her too, but don't let that mess up your head again. We made a choice, and it is about time we learn to accept it. She made her choice, and we made ours. Nabeel needs to remember his mama in good light. You need to let go."

Silence echoed in the air.

Upon receiving no response, Saud simply squeezed Eliyas's shoulder and walked away.

Eliyas had been in a foul mood for a completely different reason, but now, the reminder of another memory worsened his mood. Perhaps, this was why he was feeling extra bitter and nasty today. He didn't want to be reminded of his failures, mistakes and losses.

Feeling frustrated, he now felt the extreme need to lash out. The foulness and soaring of temper was real. He needed to get his control back.

He needed to pay his wife a little visit, terrify her a little more.

Chapter 12

E liyas

Sitting sideways on his bike, Eliyas inhaled the warm, polluted and smoke-mixed air that hovered like a cloud above the Labourer's society. This place was a shameful secret, subtly denied by Hill Land. In a highly advanced city, the smudge-covered hands and the scent of poverty were seen as a sign of disgrace.

Only the rich and powerful survived.

Sporting a half-smile and resting one foot on the seat, with his elbow resting on his knee, Eliyas kept gazing at one dirty building that stood tall in the midst of all misery and malnourishment. Sila lived in that building. The fall of a queen...he had snatched her from jewels and forced her to It was a sweet victory. Yet, there had been a sense of nostalgia.

He belonged to the streets.

One can deny, but the truth is always there...persistent; this was his reality, his home.

The smell of baked mud, sweat...the cries of starved children were almost comforting. This is what he had traded away; his truth. He wasn't ashamed. It was the survival of the fittest. To watch the rich hover above, with an arrogant gleam, he had simply snatched a few gleams.

He had hovered beneath someone else's spotlight.

"Why are you sitting here?" An old man suddenly walked up to him with a judgemental look.

People on this side of the streets had to be cautious.

Any random person could be a threat.

"I came to meet my wife." A subtle smirk filled with mischief appeared on Eliyas's face, as he momentarily looked up at the window that probably led to Sila's room.

He seemed like an admirer standing beneath his damsel's window.

How romantic!

The thought made him chuckle.

Turning to look at the man again, he was surprised to now see a soft look on the old man's face.

"It has been tough, hasn't it? This recession...I know you are telling the truth. I can see love in your eyes for that woman. It must be tough letting her live here. Where do you work?"

"Just a place..." He scratched the nape of his neck, averting his gaze while downplaying what he did.

He was only being civil right now because he respected everyone truly belonging to this side of the streets. They all seemed to be fighting the same battles.

"My son also has to stay away from us while he earns. His wife and son miss him so much. Yet, that is the price one has to pay if one wants to eat a day's meal. Just make sure you take care of your wife;

perhaps, come to visit her in the daytime." The man gave a wrinkled smile.

Eliyas could only watch with a slightly amused look.

Seemingly content with his words of wisdom, the man then began walking away...towards some open brown fields.

Love his wife...indeed.

Eyeing some young men randomly standing a few feet away from him, laughing and boasting about some race, Eliyas found a smile appear on his face.

He looked up at Sila's room window and back at the group of rowdy men. Money, it gave voice, it became handy when one wanted to send a message.

With a small smile, Eliyas began walking towards the men.

Those poor souls who had associated the feeling of love with him...

He shook his head at such level of naivety.

Rich fools.

Sila

Scorching intense eyes blazed into mine. With a warm grip on my hand, he gave me the sweetest smile. The weather was grey, windy, and there were echoes of an abyss. I was standing as his bride, as he stood with a look of pride in his eyes.

We were in the middle of the roads.

The night stars were shining...

"Please don't go. Please don't leave me alone."

"Never. You are my wife."

"I was broken before I met you. You have no idea how alone I was. Don't ever hurt me..."

"I won't."

Yet, suddenly, the memory grew dark. My own screams echoed from somewhere far. I could only listen in horror, watching the roads darken before me and feeling shackles choke my throat.

"No..."

"I am sorry, Sila. I am so sorry."

Tears rolled down my cheeks. I never knew if I was sleeping or just imagining a nightmare. I never even knew when my mind had pulled me into a state of unconsciousness. There was a hint of morning light falling into the room.

Rubbing my eyes, I felt the crust gathered in its corner and winced at their sharp sensation.

Pain...I was accustomed to it.

I was now sitting before the window, feeling my backache because of the restless sleep, and sighed as a sense of exhausation hit me hard.

It had all started as a competition.

The day I had to hide in my classroom during recess because I had no friends to hang out with, the moment the queen bee of my school, who used to verbally thrash me, got the sweetest man proposing her in front of the main gates, there was a need to be heard. I needed to be heard.

It was tiring staying in the shadows, watching everyone trample over me. My cousin, my friends...I competed to make some space between them, to fit in. I wanted to feel special, important, pretend that I deserved better when my cousins would hang out together and leave me behind, claiming they didn't invite me because I just wouldn't enjoy extrovert activities.

I had emotions, feelings...

I wanted to be adored for being me, and I guess it was impossible. All the time, when I had been blaming my cousins...today, I felt as if I was just too weak. I was. I was an easy target. I had wished for something more than my league. Because the truth was clear; it was hard for people to love someone like me. I tried, I reached out...but I was just fooling myself.

People, like me, are pushed down, blocked out and treated as losers by society. We can't compete. I had just been trying to win a race that was already won by so many. This was never a competition. Eliyas had won...everyone who had ever belittled and wronged me had won.

Feeling tears roll down my eyes again, I had to press my fist against my face to keep my cries muffled. My roommates were still sleeping. Maryam was muttering something in her sleep. In the midst of these depreciating thoughts, she was one of the few that didn't make me feel low. She treated me as an equal. I was going to lose her, too.

Today, I would resign...leave, and then what?

I had to tell this girl how grateful I was that she had decided to befriend me. The creeping sensation of loneliness had felt comfortable when I got to share it with her. Yet, now, I had to leave. Go back...

The clouds roared outside...and I knew that I was just fighting a false battle.

My cousins, families, all those who hurt me, that made me want to compete, must be in their homes-settled, loved and adored. And here, I was breaking over their words, gestures and actions.

I had destroyed myself for so many who didn't even deserve my tears.

The way my uncle had told me that I was now just an outsider for my loved ones had pierced. No one wanted me back home. My parents had never searched for me. A part of me wondered if they hated me now...if my mistakes had squeezed out a mother's love for her child. My parents adored me. Yet, now...I wondered if their anger weighed more than their love for me.

Why did I betray people who were offering me unconditional love?

To compete with my cousin, Kiran, Sumaiya, Neha..? For some sweet words? My father was just one of the many brothers living in our main house. He worked a 9-5 job, while my uncles were the ones who were truly rich. Maybe, it was my own complex to score a loving fantasy that would scream my worth. I had longed for a gasp of air while drowning in the shadows. I had crushed my own throat in the process.

Feeling a wave of sobs hit me again, I began crying again...feeling miserable at the thought that I had to keep my pain silent so that my roommates wouldn't be disturbed. It was soul-crushing to have to suppress the anxiety and grief inside of me.

However, just as I was sobbing, the room door got rudely jolted. Someone began knocking on it with what seemed like mighty fists.

"Open up!"

Dread hit me hard.

What was going on?

All girls woke up and sat straight with a shriek.

We all started exchanging confused, scared looks, as the room door was now harshly kicked.

"What is going on?" Maryam met my eyes, but I had no answer.

Dread, fear of what it could be was draining...

We were on the poverty-infested side of the streets. I moved my back to the window, frantically eyeing escape routes. However, in mere moments, the door got unhitched from the frame and harshly collapsed down on the floor.

Everyone screamed in extreme fear, springing to stand on their feet!

Four men, probably in their early twenties, were standing at the entrance. Rowdy, street men who were wearing chains, holding knives and chewing sweet paan. The sight made me feel almost faint.

"W-Who a-are y-you! W-What are y-you doing here?"

No answers!

"P-Please-"

"GO STAND IN THE CORNER!" One man harshly instructed, causing us all to immediately hurdle in one corner, hugging each other. Tears were running down my face now. This is what Eliyas had done to me. Because of him, I was staying in this horrendous place. It was all his fault.

I hated that man. I hated him so much.

I wish he went through all of this too! I wish he suffered for all he had done to me.

I hoped he suffered exactly the same way!

If these men had been sent by him to get me...I won't make it easy for him! I won't! I would never forgive that monster! I won't! Tears began blurring my vision, as I hugged my roommates. The fear of the unknown was nerve-wracking.

Would any person in this building stand up for us?

Whimpering and shivering, I listened as the men then began rudely thrashing our stuff, cutting the mattresses wide open, pushing the small stove to the ground, breaking cutlery, etc. All the hard work and effort put in thrashed in mere minutes.

Some people were heartless.

We could all just watch in despair, as our sole wealth got destroyed in mere minutes. Mercy; we wanted to beg for it. Every scratching and breaking sound crushed our own hearts. Hurdled together, as victims of this harsh society, abandoned by many...

I was a married woman.

Soon, it seemed like the men were done and were about to leave. A strange emotion of relief hit me. Finally!

However, just as they all started moving towards the exit again, one man stopped, turned towards us women and harshly scowled. "Message from Eliyas; Don't you dare leave this place! He will find you!" With that horrifying threat, the group of street gangsters left.

My eyes had rounded in horror, realization, hatred and extreme dread.

Eliyas...he was behind this...

Under the dark clouds, with the harsh wind picking up and rain pelting down, I rushed down the streets. I didn't take a taxi this morning. I wanted to run, get rid of the suffocating feeling of being a prisoner. Trapped; badly, brutally, cruelly...I was trapped. I could feel the shackled around my feet.

I used to read about this in newspapers, read online stories about the dark side of society. I thought that being a resident in a safe neighbourhood, I would never have to deal with such realities; they almost felt fictional, story-like. Yet, here, I had found myself dangled in such a dangerous mess. This wouldn't end well.

Street crimes were common and life-threatening.

Too many girls became a victim of gang crimes, dark markets, etc.

I had made one of the biggest mistakes of my life by allowing a street biker to manipulate me. I had been an easy prey! Rushing past the streets, which were empty because of the pouring rain, I kept dragging my fists across my cheeks as I ran.

He had promised me lies, and I had fallen for it...

The signs had been there.

The world had been screaming for me to be cautious, but I had ignored it all. For love, for acceptance, my rosy dreams had been snatched by him. My heart wasn't his to soil, yet I had given him the opportunity. And now, completely lost and strayed away, I was rushing down empty streets, feeling so alone.

The agony was crushing me.

Scream, cry...I was regretting the moment I allowed Eliyas to announce his lies.

With the rain pelting down, my tears felt warm against the cold. They were my heat in this storm.

To love so intensely....my love...it had failed me.

My feet were hurting, rubbing against the harsh gravel of the floor. I was wearing shoes, yet even then, I could feel the harshness of the solid ground. I could feel every sensation that gave me pain...

What was I going to do now?

Eliyas was going to show no mercy.

Upon finally reached the coloured side of the city, I kept rushing while knowing that no one would notice the broken girl. Everyone, here, were either travelling in expensive cars or had their heads covered by huge red and black umbrellas. No one was bothering with the girl who was rushing under the open sky.

This was the busy life of the city.

Feeling my heartbeat at an erratic speed, the urge to just run away growing fierce, I reached the entrance of my workplace, wiping my face, and was about to rush in with an emotion of heartfelt pain when my elbow was gripped.

Forcefully twirled around, I gasped out loud and was about to snap at the perpetrator, when I saw who it was.

Eliyas...

His jaw was clenched.

I suddenly felt so vulnerable, as he eyed my red-rimmed eyes; still holding on to my elbow. The rain was pelting down. Yet, in the midst of the roar of the weather, there was a sense of silence. He looked down at me. I stared up with an expression that cried 'why' what was he getting from doing all this?

What did I ever do to him?

He grabbed my chin harshly in between his thumb and finger, trailing his gaze over my red-rimmed eyes, pink nose, as I just watched with a tilted head, and then he allowed a small smirk to appear on his face.

"I will see you at work." He let go of me, winking mischievously and turning around to face the entrance while smoothing the creases of his designer wear. He was putting on his professional look again.

I was left completely horrified.

This was his confession...his declaration.

I couldn't leave.

This was his announcement of how he was ten steps ahead of me.

Resignation...

I had been so naive to think that he would just let me go. He wouldn't. This man had it out for me. H-He wasn't going to let me leave. He was going to make sure that I suffered, got ruined for loving him.

He wasn't willing to put his weapons down. He was seeing me as a game. I could only watch in shock as he trotted inside the building, leaving me behind-so cold, so shaken. He would drown me. He would not let go.

Now, I had no choice but to fight...

I had to free myself. And running away was no longer an option.

He wanted me to put up a fight

Wiping my face again, I sniffed loudly to compose myself and then began heading inside the building. My nerves were shaking, blood pumping straight into my ears. I couldn't run, hide...get away...my every step felt so suffocating.

I had to fight back.

Chapter 13

Sila

I was like a numb and lost worker. Moments got spent in a blur, as I performed my duties while watching the world from the back of my mind. Everything seemed like a blur. It was a locked up sensation, a rigid stance, where my soul had been pushed into a complete state of shock.

I couldn't believe my reality.

I couldn't believe all that was happening to me, that had happened to me. The extent of Eliyas's brutality...I couldn't believe how low he was willing to stoop. Every time I thought he had acted horribly, he would exceed that benchmark. There was no limit to his barbarism.

I knew how such incidences ended...

I had read newspapers about articles about what unstable obsessive men did.

It started simple but would soon morph into a crime. The sadistic need to abuse would grow tenfolds until the criminal would finally snap during one episode. I would have to pay for someone's insanity.

Sold, forgotten and just a lesson for many.

Eyes averted to the ground, feeling completely trapped and terrified, my mind was racing over ways to get out of this huge mess. I just couldn't think of anything that would work in my favour. I felt ashamed to face Maryam, made sure to stare at the ground to avoid any accidental eye contact with Eliyas and just spent the day wiping every corner of my workplace.

I was a huge mess.

Now working on the ground floor, mopping the floor in a lost and defeated manner, I yelped as someone grabbed my shoulder from behind.

"Miss," It was just one of the female workers here. "Boss has said that we can go home now." The woman smiled.

"S-Sure." The pain inside of me had ruined my self-confidence.

I couldn't speak without feeling low and tiny. My regrets, choices and mistakes had crushed me badly. I had failed myself. I felt so exhausted and defeated. I had been fighting for so long, and today, I just felt like retreating into the corners of my heart.

My strength had taken a break today.

Nodding, the lady began walking away from me. I momentarily eyed her retreating back and went back to working for a couple more minutes. It was almost twilight. The building was almost empty. The solace of the evening bit me, and I sighed.

Loneliness, I was alone.

I was so miserably alone.

With dragged feet, I then placed the cleaning equipment in the staffroom and began walking towards the exit of the building. I didn't want to go back to the place that I had been forced to call mine. I felt so ashamed, guilty...

I didn't want to face the girl, hear their accusations that it had been my fault. Maryam would support me, but my other roommate s...they would rightfully so be mad at me for bringing danger to their door. No one was willing to fight anyone else's demons. It had only been me who had foolishly decided to overlook Eliyas's damaged ways.

A street biker...

I hated my choice so much! These weren't my scars. These weren't my issues. The dark realities of the street life were Eliyas's problems. NOT MINE! THEY WERE NEVER MINE. AND I, OUT OF LOVE, OUT OF LONGING NAIVETY, MADE THEM MINE. I was such a fool; the biggest fool...I had just recked myself for love.

Feeling anger turned into a pained sigh again, I walked out of the building and onto the open streets. The public was still on the roads, busy shopping, roaming around and working. Walking down the street path, with bright light blazing on me from the open shops, I kept my gaze on the floor, only to raise it when a mother with an adorable baby walked past me.

My heart clenched.

I lowered my gaze to the ground again. In this huge world, I felt so tiny. A suppressed fantasy hit me hard. I imagined myself smiling, laughing with the man of my dreams. Pain grasped me as an unwanted thought bit me. Eliyas appeared as a good guy, one who had actually been sincere. Images of him actually adoring me, being the man I had thought he was, hit me hard, and I shook my head.

I had put him first, loved him, ignored all the signs, and he had just crushed me. Love...it can be one's biggest weakness if they love the wrong person. I had heard of all those fantasies. I had been a fool in love, and now I was walking under the open skies with no place I could call home. I couldn't go back to The Labourers' Society.

Walking, so lost and alone, I finally managed to reach one of the local parks of the city. A bench placed in one of the secluded areas of the park would do for tonight. Climbing over the small fence, I walked inside the park and just sat down on a bench that was partially hidden by the bushes, right next to a lamp pole and before the jogging track that circled around the park.

There were still a few families in the park. Children were playing and ladies were walking around. This was a ladies park. I sat down and just absently watched the families. I used to go for walks with my family too. Now, I was sure they still went on walks, but I was no longer there to enjoy those memories.

Everyone had raced far ahead of me.

"Mind if I sit here?" A woman, around my age, hopped to sit next to me.

"C-course." My voice sounded hoarse and throaty.

"Thanks." She sat down and began drinking water from her water bottle.

"It is too hot today." She seemed in a conversational mood, an energetic smile in her tone.

"It is." Seasons were just blurring moments for me now.

"I am Parnia." The girl then introduced herself.

We were both watching the scene before us. There was a little girl twirling in the garden, right next to the swings. I felt a bit worried. She was way too close to the swings, but her supposed mother was watching her from the jogging track.

"My n-name is Sila." Confidence shattered completely.

Lowest...

"Good to know. I come to jog here almost every day. What about you?" She turned to look at me with a smile.

"I j-just came here to sit." I didn't leak a tear... anything.

"Oh."

My eyes were still trained on the little girl. Suddenly, I watched in horror as the girl grew horrifying close to the swings.

She could get hurt!

My instincts took control and I jumped.

"Watch out!" I rushed towards the child and quickly scooped her before the swing could hit her.

"Be careful, sweetie..." I patted the baby's cheek with a tender and motherly expression. I always loved children.

"What is your name?" I cooed.

"Lulu." The baby shyly spoke.

The woman, watching over the girl, began rushing in my direction.

"Thank you so much for taking care of her." She rushed up to me. She seemed in her mid-thirties.

"No problem at all." I handed the baby over to the woman.

"You were so quick!" Parnia now jogged up to stand next to me.

"Yes." The woman praised. "That was great. I am actually babysitting Little Daneen, and my mother would have been furious if something had happened to her. You have been such a gem." She caressed little Daneen's cheek who placed her head in the nape of her neck.

"She is your sister?" I was surprised.

A minute later, I realized how rude I had sounded. "So s-sorry-"

"No. No..." The woman smiled, shaking her head. "My mother runs a daycare centre. Little Daneen is one of the orphans staying in our quarters. I have a special spot for this baby. I bring her along on my daily jogs, but I have never seen you around."

"She is just here to sit." Parnia playfully quipped, making the woman laugh.

"Sweet. Do you live here?"

"Umm..."

Embarrassment hit me hard.

There was shame felt...I felt inferior and lost.

"I live in the Labourer's society."

"Oh, you looked like you belong to the city. Do you have a job?" The questions had good intentions, but I just felt so embarrassed. I didn't want to be judged.

"Umm...I-"

My emotions were clear, and emotion of sympathy crossed the woman's face. "I am Nora. My mother's daycare centre also has a section that assists women from the other side of the streets. We offer a job, a quarter and food on daily basis. Would you be interested?"

A spark hit me.

Could it be?

I felt embarrassed yet eager. My self-esteem was roaring, and I didn't want to sound pathetic by claiming how much I needed this...I needed this so much!

"Course. I mean it would be g-good to get a nice bed to sleep in." I tried pulling it off as a joke but quickly winced because of the way my words sounded.

Pity; I had sounded so miserable.

My voice had sounded so broken, cracky and just desperate.

Nora simply gave me a compassionate smile."Come to this address tomorrow for a background check and interview." She then pulled out a card from her leather handbag and handed it to me.

"Is this offer also available for a friend of mine?" I asked.

Maryam had to come along, too.

I couldn't leave her behind. We needed protection and a pleasant place to stay. Terror hit me as I wondered about what Eliyas would do once I moved out of the Labourer's society. Yet, I knew he couldn't really steal me away from a commercial place.

"Come for the interview tomorrow, and we will see..." She gave me a smile that held authority.

"Of course." I immediately nodded.

Despite being grateful and sounding so sweet, Nora did have an elite edge. I realized that I had to stay formal and composed in her presence.

After ruining my back by sleeping on the stone bench, I had woken up at the sound of early morning penguins flapping their wings. Hard pain had hit me at the thought of how miserable my heart was feeling. Under the open sky, so alone, so hurt, so hungry...I felt guilty that I had kept Maryam out of the loop.

She must be so worried.

Getting up, I decided to finally get on with the day. Shivers ran. What if my absence at the workplace caused Eliyas to fume and snap; sell me? I hated how vulnerable and terrified that emotion made me.

With a mind completely boggled with fear, I moved to get myself prepared. If I managed to pass the interview, I could get some secure place. Snatching me from the roads wouldn't be so easy. There was this anxious sense of hope, and I finally willed myself to fight back.

I could do this...

"You will help the ladies take care of some children at the daycare centre." A helping lady at the centre exclaimed, showing me around. She was going to be my new boss now.

We were standing in the middle of one of the halls assigned to cater for some of the children. I had my interview and was immediately given the job. I was even told that I could recommend one of my friends for a vacancy here. I felt so emotional. I couldn't wait to share this with Maryam.

A new job, a secure place to stay...no need to face Eliyas on daily basis.

I would hide away in this place until Eliyas forgot about me or decided I wasn't worth all the effort.

My new job was a level beneath working at Kingston Inc, but at least, it was going to provide me with some freedom. My heart clenched at what exactly Nora had offered me to become; a low wage working staff member.

Memories hit me hard.

"You will become our family doctor." My grandma gushed, squeezing my cheeks.

"She will. She can have our clinic." Mama added with pride in her tone.

"And I will treat people for free." The twelve-year-old me was naive.

So many dreams, a plan, and all thrown in the drain because of one choice.

"Here," The lady pushed a little baby boy in my direction. He was the first one to arrive at this place. Looking hardly one year old, the boy had the sweetest smile and was fast asleep.

I found it strange how this lady was willing to hand over a baby to a trainee, yet non the less, I grabbed the baby.

"He is so cute." I cradled, running a finger over his round cheek.

"Yeah, he is. The babysitters will come in an hour. I have-"

"My son, Nabeel, was just dropped off here. I am here to tak-"

A chilling sensation, the voice heard so many times, yet there was dread. So much dread. No, he couldn't. It couldn't be. H-He had already done so much. Not this...

Yet, the truth was in front of me.

Eliyas, looking powerful, had stepped into the hall.

Son?

He had a son?

I looked down at the sleeping baby with so much dread, pain and horror.

Son?

"What the heck! WHAT ARE YOU DOING HERE? Holding my baby! WHO HANDED HIM TO YOU?"

Terror shook me.

Yet, I was in a complete state of shock. Everything seemed blurry, numb...Like I had zoned out of my mind, watching from where behind.

Lost, the fight in me was completely lost.

"Sir," The lady tried to pacify, yet Eliyas was having none of it as he stomped his way towards me.

I could only watch in numb fatigue as he snatched the baby from me, yelling at the staff lady. She was explaining that I had been newly hired here. Both of them headed out of the hall, leaving me behind completely shattered.

He had a son, a family.

He had snatched me from my family.

A mother's daughter...he had made me break my mother's heart. I had broken my mother's heart.

Empty arms could only feel the weight of what had been stolen from them.

I stood in the same posture, wondering, dreading if this was being to be a circular pattern for me. Eliyas would steal all opportunities. Everything!

His son was adorable.

He had love!

Chapter 14

- -

S ila

Warm eyes, sweetest smiles...such a beautiful gift.

My feet had rushed away and sunk down on the floor in sheer misery.

I had lost. I had lost myself.

Speechless, wordless...when it all started, I had no clue. I had no idea where I could cry, grieve or hide. A shattering heartbreak, it hurt...it hurt so much.

How did I allow myself to break so easily?

How did I give one person to hurt me this much?

Struck by a storm yet still standing and watching it destroy me. There was a sensation of shock, utter emotion of loss. Everything seemed hard now, draining...

There was also a sense of dejection, suffocation. I had no reason to complain, to blame because I had allowed this to happen to me. I had allowed myself to get crushed over and over again by a dream. I had seen people get cured by love, heard such great love stories, yet the only thing 'love' ever did to me was break me.

I had seen finest tales, dreamt fine stories, yet here I was...alone, while the person who had once owned my heart had his heart filled with the warmth of his adorable son, a possible family. It hurt. It hurt so much. There were just so many thoughts.

Did he have a wife when conning me?

Was he madly heads or heels for someone?

Did he actually have a heart that loved yet didn't melt for me?

The blew to my self-esteem was just huge. He had used me. He had fooled me! There was a part of me that used to see Eliyas as just a cruel man, but now knowing that he did know how to love just made me feel like a failure.

I had been so naively swayed by the cliche of a street biker turning good for the shy introvert.

This man was simply not interested.

It was appalling to think that men with families could hurt others so brutally.

Eliyas just saw me as an opportunity.

I didn't get kicked from my new job, instead, I was made to stay and watch the horrible antics of my husband. Eliyas had tried his best to get me removed, kicked to the curb, but the institute resisted against such a demand. They claimed that I would be appointed to another section of the daycare and won't be allowed near Nabeel.

It was a bluff.

Eliyas threw the worst accusations in my direction, claimed that he won't allow a girl from some unknown background to be near his son, would soon move his baby to a better institute, but the institute decided to favour me. The shell of me was 'supposedly' offered some sympathy, but crushing reality struck when I realized why such a privilege was offered; the institute needed cheap labour.

It was a rollout of pain; strick three striking me so many times.

I had been given a minute-size room to stay in, there had been no real discussion about payment in solid numbers, and I was offered saline water. Fool, that was my new vibe. People just saw me as a fool now. Nora, she had seen my vulnerable side as an opportunity and struck, yet this time I did not mind being a fool.

Eliyas was making me feel resilient with the chance of working as a bought slave.

Every time, I felt like he had stooped to his lowest level, he would do more. There was a notion of a heartwrenching cry echoing inside of me, yet I couldn't utter a peep. All my dreams had been crushed and spewed right in front of me.

Eliyas had done more than just destroy me. His anger had also led to him punishing someone I held so dear to me; Maryam.

I had resigned from my old workplace and seen the destruction that was caused by my choices.

Back in our room, Maryam and I met.

There was shame and guilt with which I had explained my absence, but to my horror, that was the least of my worries. Sitting near the window, Maryam had revealed the bitter truth, making me regret ever allowing this girl near me.

"He will provide me a home." Her smile had been rueful, adjusted in her situation.

"M-Maryam, n-no, we can move now. The daycare centre caters to weak women. H-he won't be able to reach us. I am so sorry for putting you in such a situation. I am so sorry for what Eliyas did. Come with me-" I was desperate, almost hysterical.

"I c-can't." Her eyes were full of tears, head lowered. "This is my chance. I am so sorry for being this selfish." She met my gaze with so much pain and devastation. I realized the damage that had been done.

It was all my fault.

Money had been such a manipulative bait.

My eyes welled up in my own emotion of devastation and guilt.

One of the goodhearted elderly men at our workplace, a friend of Eliyas, needed a young wife. Eliyas had suggested Maryam's name who was then proposed.

Sobs...deep and agonized sobs were parading inside of me.

"I-I a-am so sorry, Maryam...so sorry." We hugged, and the realization that Eliyas had stolen another moment of my life was brutal. In his cruelty, he was willing to destroy another girl's life.

I couldn't do anything about it.

A friend gone, pushed back...I could no longer meet Maryam because I couldn't take a lot of chances roaming outside the premises of my new home. I was afraid that Eliyas would snatch me from the streets. My fears made me feel like a coward. Fortunately, none of my other roommates was strangely mad at me. In fact, they were glad that I was choosing to leave.

Emotions had brimmed.

Would I ever get to meet Maryam again?

My one true friend in this crisis...she was going to pay for my choices. I couldn't save her.

"I wish you the very best for your future. I wish so much for you. You were there for me when so many had turned their backs. Thank you so much for all that you did for me." Words. I could only offer words.

"No. Thank youuu. I hope you find your happiness as soon as possible." And that was the end of it.

Simple.

It had felt like one chapter had ended. Two travellers had moved on with their own journeys. I was squished with the intense feeling of loss and being left behind. We had promised to stick together.

We had planned to climb out of our miseries together.

Now, in my new home, I was breathing in the constant pain of disbelief, anger and numbness. How could I ever make Eliyas pay? How could I ever make this man regret crushing me in this ruthless manner? How could I make him pay for hurting Maryam?

I wanted to do so much, but I couldn't. Like a bought slave, I would work; day and night-just to blank out my miseries.

"Wipe the floors quickly." One of the babysitters rudely barked at me, as I now worked in the Hall B of the institute. There were just so many children, and hardly 5-6 babysitters taking care of them.

I was given the duty to take care of cleaning the floors, several halls and helping the babysitters at all times. Many of them would actually dump all of their duties on me. It was so strange, so suspicious. The way things happened here was strange. Yet, I couldn't raise my queries.

"Here," the babysitter, hardly out of her teens, handed me a sleepy baby girl and then began walking out of the hall while talking to her husband on the phone. She had recently got married.

Some girls just knew how to make a man stay.

Simply shaking my hand at the girl's antics, I cradled the baby girl in my arms, while zoning out the noise of crying babies and toddlers around me, and smoothed a finger over the baby's round cheeks. So chubby, cute and Asian...she was so adorable.

Babies were such a blessing.

My eyes squeezed shut for a moment in a notion of sharp pain, my heart clenched, as I pondered over how lucky Eliyas was to have such a gift. He was just so lucky! So darn lucky!

"Hush..." I cooed, as the baby girl began whimpering in her sleep. "Hush...sweetie." I began rocketing her, hugging her so close to me.

The bright sun was blazing into the hall from its wall-length windows.

The moment felt heartwarming.

"Shh..." I caressed her cheeks adoringly.

"Why are you holding the baby?" A stern voice suddenly interrupted me, making me look up in shock. It was one of the senior babysitters; Mrs Chaudry. She was in her early forties and was the incharge of this hall.

"Ummm..." I felt embarrassed. "Naila told me to-"

"Of course." Mrs Chaudhry rolled her eyes, clearly aware of Naila's antics.

"Just go and place the baby on the playing rug. I will take care of her," she ordered, turning around and moving across the floor to check how others were doing. I felt oddly scolded.

It hurt how I couldn't be trusted with a child here. It made sense, yet still, it was just a crushing thought. I love children.

"Okay, then." Sniffing, feeling already too broken to feel anything more, I was about to head towards the playing rug when one of the other cleaning ladies who had been wiping the floor a few feet away from me suddenly moved up to me.

"Don't take it to your heart, kiddo." She kept wiping the floor, painfully reminding me of the times that I had been in the position of Eliyas's office floor. How humiliating! "Mrs Chaudhry might be strict, but this hall is way better than so many other sections of this place. You have no idea what goes around in the other halls."

"What goes around?" I frowned, eyeing Mrs Chaudhry cautiously, just to make sure that she didn't start walking in my direction again.

The woman looked hesitant for a second and then spoke in a conspicuous tone, "Acts that can almost be classified as a crime. It is surprising that such a prestigious place has such a lousy system. You have no idea how horrible the other babysitters are. They have an advantage that these babies can't really speak."

What the heck!

Disgust and uneasiness struck me hard.

"Really?" Eyes wide and in denial.

"Yes..." She nodded, hushing me.

I found it so hard to digest.

Nora had seemed a generous and loving lady. Despite her mother exploiting the working class, I thought the babies were well taken care of, but could it really be? Was this place actually harbouring an atmosphere of negligence?

The poor babies, I felt so horrified.

"W-What exactly did they do?" I asked stunned.

"Negligence, digging in their lunch, I am not really sure, but they are rough with the kids. I think the admin knows." There was sorrow and guilt in her tone, making my heart sink.

"B-but why doesn't anyone do anything about it?" My voice cracked, not believing how conveniently people were managing to get away with this dysfunctional atmosphere.

This was inhumane.

"Can we really?" She raised her eyebrows in a knowing manner, causing my shoulders to slump down in the most tortured manner.

"Ummm...I-I-" I didn't know what to say,

The anguish was real.

It was power versus the weak. Again!

"I-I need a break." Suddenly, I was just feeling so exhausted.

Hugging the baby tight, I then asked the woman to place the baby girl on the playing rug and began heading towards the exit of the hall. The cries of the babies echoing in the air had abruptly turned so heartbreaking and traumatic.

"Course." The woman understood my need.

Crystal skies were so clear and bright.

There were people walking around in the vast gardens. Faded colours...everything just felt so deflated like I was being paraded down by the shackles shoved on my shoulders.

The world used to seem warmer from behind the shadows.

Men with cold hearts, women that supposedly had no warmth for children...I was helplessly witnessing it all. I didn't want to face this side. I didn't want to witness the dark side of this society. Ignorance had been so blissful. Yet, now I was learning so much.

How could I tolerate staying in a place that had such disturbing rumours floating in the air? Was this the reason Nora had offered me a place here? To keep the institute's ways safe?

I didn't know what to believe. The cleaning lady could just be gossiping, but still, the thought was disturbing. This place wasn't as friendly as I had hoped.

Everywhere I looked, someone was getting preyed upon by the powerful. I didn't know how to fight against it, how to rebel against this.

Frustrated, I couldn't think of any outlet. I was taking favour from a place that was 'allegedly' cruel.

What was I supposed to do?

I wasn't sure how truthful the helping lady had been...the level of misconduct taking place in this place. I wonder what I would do if I was to witness a child getting mistreated. My conscience would destroy me if I did nothing. I had left my old work for this. I would be out of options if I did nothing, but I wouldn't tolerate someone hurting children.

Again, I was trapped.

So confused and frustrated, I began heading back towards the hall when I saw a lady walking out of another hall while carrying a crying baby in her arms. She had a vicious scowl on her place while she was roughly trying to rock the baby to sleep. It was Nabeel.

Somehow, I rushed in his direction.

"May I?" I fearfully asked, hoping she hadn't been informed that I had to stay away from this baby.

"Course." She dumped Nabeel in my arms and began drinking soda from the bottle she had been carrying in her right hand. This was the security level here.

Shaking my head at this, I lowered my head to gaze down at Nabeel and felt an emotion grip me hard.

He had Eliyas's eyes.

He was crying, screaming, and his tears were worrying me.

"Hush, little baby." I cupped his cheek. "It is alright. I am here. I am here." I cooed, causing him to momentarily stop in between his sobs and stare at me curiously. So innocent, so cute...his round eyes were looking at me with so much need. My heart broke.

I could take this baby away. I could steal this baby. This was my chance. I could finally hurt Eliyas. I wanted to. I wanted to take something super precious from him. He stole me from my parents. This was my chance. My perfect chance to finally avenge my ruination. But, I didn't.

Drops of tears fell off the baby's cheeks, as I held him...lowly crying while peering down at him. He suddenly gave me a smile. A smile that wiped away all of my furious thoughts and made me hug him tight. This precious child...this baby...his father was a horrible man, but this smile was all I needed.

One innocent and pure smile...I had needed that so much.

I hugged baby Nabeel tightly, so tightly with a sense of protection.

One day, one day, Eliyas would regret it all. One day, but Nabeel...I won't wish him any hard.

Not today, never.

Chapter 15

Sila

Pain...there are moments where you see others breathing in smiles and you realize that not everyone gets a taste of depression. Everyone has their share of tales, scars behind glittery facades, but in your pain, you just see others living fairytales, floating. When drowning, every floating one is noticed instead of focusing on the sunk ones.

I was drowning.

Breathless, pressure so gripping on me, hands reaching out in desperation but finding no hand to grab on. This is what depression felt like. Bitter. insane...retreated to the anxious parts of my heart. And strangely, my moments of smiles arrived when I would get to meet Nabeel. The little baby had the sweetest smile-so innocent and pure. It was a gift.

"Hush, sweetie," I gushed, allowing him to hold two of my fingers in his tiny fists.

It was lunchtime, and I had slipped out of Hall B to visit this baby. Any moment, he would be taken away from this place. In fact, he hardly stayed at this place for an hour or two. I knew that Eliyas won't let Nabeel stay in this place for long; this is how horrible minds thought.

Everyone was a threat or danger for crude people. They believed that everyone had the capability to stoop low. I was actually surprised why Eliyas was even allowing Nabeel to stay at this place for an hour or two. It was quite confusing.

Anyhow, no matter, what Eliyas was thinking, I knew that I could never stoop down to his level of nastiness.

This was my husband's son.

Sighing, while taking in broken breaths of vulnerability, my days turned into a routine-a routine that I was again following today.

The babysitter had brought Nabeel out for a walk in the gardens and I had intervened. There were hardly a few people outside. Somehow, it was a lonely part of me that sought out for longed emotions. This baby's father had hurt me. I wanted to remain in the bubble where I had an upper hand, where I did good in exchange for bad.

"Nabeel..." I pinched the baby's cheek, as the babysitter allowed me to hold him. The sun was blazing hot. The babysitter handed me Nabeel's milk bottle and then moved behind some bushes to talk on her phone. So many employees did that here.

If this was how reputed daycares managed things, I wonder what the condition of the low-level daycares was. It was horrible to think how insensitive people could be. Yet, this time, I wasn't surprised.

Rocking Nabeel and caressing his cheeks with the palm of my hands, feeling my tears tickle down on his cheeks every now and then, I watched as he simply gave me smiles, gargling randomly and making happy noises.

He liked me.

"Aww...Nabeel, you are the cutest baby ever." I was having a heart-to-heart confession with a baby. "Your father...he has hurt me so much." It was like a catharsis to me; rant it all out to the son of my oppressor. "He has hurt me, and he has you. I wish I had you! Sweet baby...I wish no harm comes to you, that you never have to pay for your father's actions." People were cruel for contaminating children with toxicity.

Sweetest beans crushed by some monsters of our society. No child was a killer, murder, etc..it was society that turned innocent minds into sinister beings. It was the society that didn't even spare children/

I didn't want that to happen to Nabeel. I didn't want yet another innocent person to become a victim of Eliyas's viciousness. I knew Eliyas would raise his son the same manner he had been raised. Those moral values, customs...this little baby would be told to break and snatch, and it was just painful thinking about how this sweetest baby would soon be breaking hearts and destroying homes.

Agony hit me hard.

"I hope and pray that you don't turn out like him." I cooed, brushing Nabeel's cheek in a rather depressed manner, I knew that there was a high chance that he would turn out to be like his father...or mother.

"Here, Nabeel..." I then began making him drink milk, watching his look curiously at me with wide eyes. He frowned, as I tried to coax him into grabbing his feeder.

He didn't like lunchtime.

It was strange how this baby would take time to drink milk. He would get irritated. try to push it away, but after a few tries, he would drink it. Today, he was doing the same, and a strange sense of uneasiness was felt.

"Nabeel..." He had slight tears in his eyes, breaking my heart.

Oh, baby...

Something was wrong. Something was horribly wrong.

I poured a drop of milk on hand, smelling it, tasting it. It tasted fine, but still...this baby was just not enjoying his milk. It seemed something more than being lactose intolerance. Concern hit me hard.

This institute was too unpredictable, too unreliable...

It was time I investigated this matter.

I couldn't inform Eliyas because he would crush me even before I managed to get a peep out, so I had to take matters into my own hands. Until Nabeel was being kept here, I had to make sure that he was safe.

Eliyas

"Saud, it has been a week. Did you find a new daycare centre?"

"I am searching. His current one is the best in town."

"I don't care." Irritation filled Eliyas's tone. "Nabeel needs a proper daycare, and I need to get back to my work." He screeched on the phone.

"Look...I know you do. But, it is just taking time. I am asking around. Some agencies have recommended a few." Saud's tone was stressed. It seemed as if he was driving around the streets.

Eliyas rubbed his face in annoyance, clenching his mobile phone tightly in his hands, as he stared outside his office's window.

This had been a routine lately.

While Eliyas worked, he would leave Nabeel in Saud's care. He could hardly focus on his work, only attend meetings, being concerned about the unstable routine of his son. Nabeel needed a proper daycare, not to spend his mornings on the roads.

Though Eliyas was paying Saud for taking care of his son, he knew that even Saud would not put his routine on hold for long. It was just how things worked here.

Fury grew!

Sila...that woman! Eliyas would crush her for this!

Her audacity...he was furious that Nabeel's previous headquarter had managed to side with her. That desperate woman!

FINE!

If she even took a step out of that place now, he was going to dump her at Don's. He would get his money share in the exchange for selling her. She was creating issues now. He didn't have patience or time for that.

'Just bring Nabeel to me now. I am free." Eliyas then breathed in, trying to cool his temper, as he leaned back against his office chair and closed his eyes,

"I will take cash right now."

"I know."

There was not much that came free in this side of the world. People didn't even trust others with time. 'Now' was the most preferred for making payments. Saud was his closest friend, but both of them knew that it was never wise to trust others when it came to money.

It had always been this way.

They had grown up together, learned these lessons together, bandaged each other's wounds, cheered, bucked each other up in their lows, but money was a line that they both never crossed. It would only be foolish to trust one on that.

"Okay. I will reach your office in half an hour." Saud beams, causing Eliyas to frown.

Before he could question why so long, the call ended.

Suspicion grew.

Saud was taking too long in searching for a new daycare centre, and Eliyas was well-aware of how attractive easy money was. It was time to get the reigns back in order

Flipping his laptop open, he decided to make a few quick calls via Skype. He was personally going to talk to the agencies.

Clock ticked.

Half-an-hour has passed.

An unknown sensation hit him, the feeling of discomfort and irritation. Something wasn't right. He fidgeted on his office seat, focusing on his laptop while a strange sensation was still filling his heart-an agitating emotion, suffocating feeling.

His mobile phone rang, causing him to immediately swipe against its screen and press it against his ear.

"Saud, where the heck are you!"

"E-Eliyas..." A sobbing feminine voice spoke instead, chilling his heart with dread and fury.

"Sila?"

Why the heck was she calling him?!

That woman...

A strange form of dread, confusion and anger was fully hitting him now.

"H-He had an allergic reaction to something put in the milk, so t-they gave him some medicine. He has fainted, and t-they are trying to keep it wraps, treat him on their o-own." She kept on sobbing, hiccuping and in complete hysterics.

She had always been so vulnerable, soft and weak.

"Who?" Her sobs were irritating him, but his attention was solely focused on her words. The feeling of suffocation and discomfort had grown even more profound. He didn't want to hear it. He didn't want to hear it at all. Blanched, he didn't want to hear how much of a fool he had been. His voice sounded hollow, terrified, numb.

"Nabeel. I secretly took your number and called you! Please come!"

Muscles tightened.

The feelings had been true, warning him of horrors.

He didn't want to believe it. He didn't want to accept what he had heard.

His son, the reason he was at working so hard, striving so hard for normalcy, the one for whom he was evening willing to destroy...he didn't want to even think that his son was suffering.

"I am coming." A clenched jaw, fists curled...he didn't allow Sila to get even a single peek at his emotions.

Immediately getting up, he began thundering his way outside his office. He wasn't going to spare Saud for this. He wasn't going to spare that leeching institution. If any harm came to his son, he would spill blood.

"It was this woman; Sila. She was the one who was secretly feeding him milk. She was the one secretly going near him." Accusations had started.

The owners had been called in.

The police had been called in.

The institution had been thrown into a state of panic and havoc, as Eliyas had stormed inside it. His baby had been lying so helplessly in one of the health rooms. So many of the staff members had gathered around him, including Sila.

They all had turned blanched at the sight of Eliyas and stepped aside from the suffering baby, who was now half-faint, crying and wailing in pain.

Rage hit Eliyas hard.

He quickly rushed to Nabeel, picking him up, looking horrified by the sight.

His Nabeel...what had they done to him?

What had Sila done to him!

She had called him! Was it fear, dread...acceptance of her crime?

"You disgusting woman! You dare even go near my son! See what I am going to do with you now! Just wait!" He screeched, glaring ferociously in the direction of Sila and taking one step closer to her, while she looked so scared and terrified. She was shaking her head in denial, bawling out loud, but Eliyas didn't even wait for any explanations.

Rushing to his car, he quickly turned the ignition. His Nabeel...t emper soon replaced extreme fear. His son...his baby...he kept the hold tight on his son, as he frantically broke signals to reach the hospital.

Nabeel was still wailing, crying, yet seemed so drowsy now.

If anything happened to his son, he would never forgive himself.

Saud...Eliyas didn't even want to think about how much a traitor that man was.

Speeding, he finally reached the hospital and left his car in the ignition, as he jumped out of his car, holding Nabeel tightly in his hands and rushed inside the hospital emergency ward.

Nurses and doctors immediately rushed in his direction. They grabbed Nabeel from his arms and began rushing him to a hospital wardroom.

"Sir, don't worry. We will take care of it." A nurse spoke.

"Just tell us what happened."

"Allergic reaction..." He urgently informed, terror and fear consuming him completely.

With a nod, the nurses rushed Nabeel towards a hospital bed, as the doctor began examining him.

He had experienced a dread similar to this when Noreen was in the hospital. Now that feeling seemed to have increased by ten folds. He had been careless. He had been arrogant and foolish, and now his son was paying for the consequences of his actions.

He shouldn't have trusted Saud.

He shouldn't have been so careless.

Sila...that woman had crossed all limits by doing this.

He should have dumped her at Don's, cashed her out the very day he married her. And now, his own choices were making him feel so regretful.

He kept hovering over his baby's bed, watching with worried eyes as the doctors worked to ease Nabeel's pain. They checked his temperature, gave him medicine and injected him with some strong doses.

Soon after painful and excruciating hours of watching Nabeel sob, he sighed with relief as Nabeel finally drifted to sleep.

"What happened?" He put his son lovingly in his arms, nudging his cheeks, as he sat down on the bed while making sure not to disturb the Branula that was inserted on Nabeel's tiny fist. The sight of his son in pain was breaking his heart.

"Allergic reaction. He is stable now, but we will be keeping him here overnight. We can move you guys to one of our rooms if you want." The doctor offered.

Relief hit him hard.

"Yes. Arrange that for me."

"Of course. Also, just so you know, you brought him here just in time. A few minutes late, and we would have been in serious trouble." The doctor gave him a relieved smile, causing him to wince. He didn't want to think what would happen if he was late.

"Thank you..." It was an uncomfortable moment, the feeling of owing another.

"My pleasure."

Rocking his baby tightly in his arms, he then leaned back against the headboard of the bed, now tiredly watching at other patients around him. He hadn't been able to focus on it before. So many sick, so many wounded...so many suffering...

However, just as he was about to fall asleep, his mobile phone rang, which immediately made Nabeel whimper in his sleep.

Darn!

Carefully placing Nabeel on the bed, Eliyas quickly looked at his phone. It was a call from the police station. He was glad they had finally called. Now that his son was alright, he was going to deal with the ones behind harming his son.

"Sir-"

"Have the owner and one of their helping ladies, Sila, been arrested? They are responsible for poisoning my son!" He barked into the phone, going straight to the point. He had his own plans for Saud.

"Sir, about that, we are still investigating the matter. If we get any information, we will surely let you know. We need to ask some questions."

"In the morning. I am still at the hospital with my son."

"Of course. We will call you if there is any further development in the case. Regards."

Eliyas simply swiped the call shut.

The feeling of horror was again getting replaced by extreme temper and fury. How dare did anyone even think of messing with his son! Saud, Sila...the very day Nabeel was getting out of this hospital, he was going to take that woman straight to Don. He was going to get his share of the money. He had been too lenient, too reckless.

He was going to make her rot jails and then sell her.

She would regret ever thinking about messing with his son!

He won't spare!

Chapter 16

S ila
Shackles scared me. Empty grey corridors horrified me. My choices seemed weak for others, but I still had no regrets about doing what I had done. It was all about choices again. This time, I wasn't concerned about the scars I would in return.

I had to save a baby.

It was horrifying seeing Nabeel turn almost blue while the crude nurses had tried to shush him. Instantly, I made the choice. I was miserable, anyways...so far from my home, everyone. Fighting for scraps thrown by the sinister ones wasn't worth allowing a baby to get hurt.

Maybe, this was my weakness...care, feeling too many emotions and allowing others to use that against me.

I should have steeled my heart, spared no second glance for the son of the man who deserved only my hate. So much hate. I should have seen his son's suffering as something he deserved. Cruel hearts needed to be broken, scarred and pushed from their thrown until they realized what they were doing to others...until they felt the pain that they had inflicted on others.

Yet, I had again melted.

With those round eyes, chubby cheeks and innocent smiles, Nabeel was just so pure and innocent baby. I could let that baby get hurt because of his father's ways. I made my choice, felt extreme worry for that boy...and then again found myself horribly punished by the crude and heartless ways of Eliyas.

Whimpering, weak and cold, I had been left sitting in a creepy police station for hours. Harsh questions, crude words, the police had been ruthless with their investigation because they knew that I had no power to protest against it.

"I was just taking care of him." My only defence.

Hands folded, gaze hardly being able to move up from the shabby table, I could only quietly whisper out my defence. There was no point in saying more. Feelings, caring, it had been my own choice.

"The institute is claiming that you had been barred from going near that child, that you hold a grudge against his father. That holds a motive."

"I didn't poison him. He was-"

"Nonsense. That institute has been running for decades-the best in town. So many children are kept there. This is the first time such a case emerged. Even the boy's father claims that you were behind it."

Eliyas...

The scorching hot feeling of strong regret was profound again.

I curled my fists, trying to control my temper, as I simply decided to stay quiet. There were so many emotions, so much anger and a nauseating spin of depression. This was horrible.

One step forward and simply dragged back...

Lesson: never show mercy to a street rat.

The weak and humiliated side of me had thought that saving Nabeel might also get Eliyas to be a bit remorseful, guilty about the way he had treated me....but instead, he had just used me as the easy punching bag. I was too tired to even cry now.

There was no point in crying anymore.

I felt like every second I was just tugging more terror and humiliation towards me, going in a downward spiral direction. Depression had hit me hard. I was just messing everything up now.

Home left behind, Maryam moving on, becoming a scapegoat for a corrupt institution, I wasn't doing anything right. I was at a low point. Hot tears had brimmed my eyes, but I was just too tired to cry them out.

Another bullseye that had destroyed me more.

However, after hours of feeling scared, overwhelmed and tired, I had finally found myself being rescued. The worker lady at the institute, the one who knew about the horrors, had finally confessed that I was innocent, that the institute was involved with some rotten business.

Discarded wrappers of sleeping pills had been found in the garbage cans of the institute.

I was let go of with a warning to stay in town.

Where...I still had no clues where I was going to stay now.

However, along with the panic of looking for a place to stay, there was also a begrudging notion of worry, concern felt for the baby with whom I had gotten attached.

It was so foolish getting attached to that child...but when did our hearts ever work on logic?

Sighing, I looked at the midnight moon and shivered as the cold wind shuddered my senses.

Embraced by the silver lines...I was the biggest fool.

Eliyas

It was after midnight when Eliyas had got another call from the police station. He had been sleeping on one of the hospital room's beds, alongside his son, when the call had jolted him awake. He wasn't really asleep, but it was one of those restless slumbers where tension and anger lingered in the back of the mind. He had fallen asleep while resting his back against the headboard of the bed, arm placed on the mattress, above his son's head.

Nabeel had been looking uncomfortable and stressed in his sleep. Eliyas was doing his best to soothe his son's pain, but there had been something discomforting Nabeel. Eliyas had called the night doctor more than a dozen times to check if something was bothering his son, but the doctors had assured him it was just the medication.

However, just as the mobile bell rang, Nabeel woke up and began crying loudly.

Anxiety and worry grew!

Something was really bothering his son!

"Nabeel..." Eliyas quickly picked his son in his arms, anxiety running through his veins.

His son was crying with so much pain, thick tears were rolling down Nabeel's cheeks.

What the heck was going on!

Sila, Saud...mad fury grew again, but there was no point in wasting time on that emotion right now. His son needed help. Urgently, he called the doctors. Something had happened to his son. Sila had done something horrible to his son.

Soon, a doctor and a nurse came rushing into his room.

"Sir-"

"My son is in so much pain. What is going on?" Eliyas wildly spoke with mad worry, anxiously swinging his baby in his hands as the doctor instantly moved to grab Nabeel from him.

"It might be a reaction to the medicine. Let's lay him down on the bed while I check," the doctor urgently spoke, rushing Nabeel to the bed.

Eliyas couldn't help constantly tugging on his locks as he now hovered over the hospital bed. This had been all his fault. He had wanted so much for his son...so much, but he had been so careless.

He still couldn't understand why Saud would make such a blunder. Raised together on dirty streets and barred knuckles, there was an odd sense of support, but Eliyas should have known better; streets rats were known to bite hands that fed them.

Striking the hands of blood ones was a norm here.

He, himself, was one such rat.

"He is fine now. We have given him painkillers and a sleeping dose. Let him rest now. We will again check his vials in the morning," The doctor assured, finally getting up, as Nabeel was finally put to sleep.

Weakened by the stress, Eliyas tiredly nodded.

The doctors left, and he, too, felt like he needed fresh air. It was so disheartening to watch his son in so much pain and stress. He had been willing to bleed his own knuckles so that his son could get everything that he hadn't been able to enjoy when he was little. It had all gone in vain.

He felt so frustrated.

Walking outside the room and closing the door with the lightest touch, He stepped out on the darkened hallway, wincing as his mobile phone rang again. He pulled it out of his pocket.

It was a call from the police station again.

This time, the determination grew firm.

He had been wanting to pend this matter till the morning, wanting to let no other interfere in his time with Nabeel. Yet, this wasn't something that could be left pending. The way Nabeel had cried, the way his son had shed so many helpless tears, he was no longer going to spare anyone a minute. He would make sure that the ones behind this would be punished as soon as possible.

"Tell me if you have made arrests already?" He sneered into the phone, not bothering about who was on the other side.

"Some of the institute staff has been brought into custody. We are calling to inform you that one of the suspects you mentioned has turned out to be innocent."

"What-"

"One of the employees of the institution confessed that Sila, the employee you mentioned, was actually trying to look after the baby. The employee has revealed that the institute was involved in mistreating children. We found medicine wrapper scraps inside the institute's trash can. Several other employees are coming forward with similar stories of witnessing abuse. We are still investigating, and rest assured...we will soon punish the true perpetrators behind this act of crime."

"BUT SHE WAS THE ONE WHO WAS FEEDING MY SON POI-SONED MILK!" Eliyas barked in disbelief, not believing what he was hearing. Sila innocent? If that woman truly believed that she could get away with this with the help of her friends, she was truly foolish. He would crush her with his own hands if he had to.

"She wasn't." The police officer calmly rebutted. "It was actually the kitchen staff that would give the feeder to your son's babysitter. We have checked, and it seems like the staff has been lacing food with a dosage of sleeping pills to keep the children asleep and easy to manage. We are still conducting further investigations; have brought in the owners and management for questions. We will let you know if there are any developments in the case."

Stunned...Eliyas didn't know what to say.

"Okay." He couldn't offer any other response.

The officer bid him goodbye and ended the call.

Moments of pure silence and disbelief spread.

He couldn't understand.

It made no sense.

Why would that woman...?

He ran his fingers through his hair, slumping against the wall, feeling totally baffled, irritated and shocked until he heard light steps entering the corridor.

Immediately looking to his left, he was caught completely off-guard by the sight before him.

What on earth!

"Shoot!" Sila had cupped her face in terror. It seemed as if she hadn't wanted to be seen. Yet, she was here. Despite everything, she was here.

Why was she here?

"What are you doing here?" He stood up straight, stress and anxiety weighing on his shoulder finally finding an outlet for lashing out. "If you are here to gloat or something, I will-" His temper was on the verge of bursting out.

She might have been innocent, but she had motives; take care of his son and get an upper hand.

He wouldn't let her take advantage of his vulnerability.

However, before he could put her in his place, a scowl immediately appeared on her face.

"Shut up! Just shut up!" She finally snapped, interrupting him, clenching her fists, looking as if she was done with his threats.

He stopped stunned, watching her with a wide expression.

What the heck!

"Are you-"

"No. Just no!" She raised her palm, ignoring his taken-back and baffled expressions. "If you think I am here for you, or even sparing you a minute of my life on you now, you are dead wrong." Her words were straight and sharp.

He stood shook.

She had always looked so terrified, so weak and feeble.

This was the first time he was seeing this wild and enough-is-enough look in her eyes, like a woman who had nothing more to lose, like someone whom he couldn't terrify with threats and power. It was a strange look on her. It didn't suit her at all.

She looked too feral, standing in the middle of the dark corridor, spilling her emotions out.

It was an intense sight.

He couldn't help but stare in silence.

"You are a disgusting man. You are horrible, corrupt, and I regret marrying you!" she spewed, not bothering if anyone heard. The corridor had no other person walking across it, but even then, she seemed like she didn't care if anyone heard. "I regret even sparing you a glance because men like you don't deserve love."

Love...what a weak insult...

"You can throw me away, sell me..." She was on a roll. "But I am done with your disgusting personality. Threaten me all you want. The only reason I am here is that, for some strange reason, I care about your son." Her confession stunned him, made him narrow his gaze.

Care? Why would she?

"He deserves a better family; love." She seemed to be pouring out her heart's content. So many words were just spilling out, and Eliyas was just shocked to stop her. "I didn't want to say this, but I hope Nabeel's pain teaches you something. The way you ruined me, took me away from my family...I hope your son doesn't suffer because of your choices. You should hope and pray that the pain you gave me doesn't impact your son's life," she finished her outburst so ruthlessly, so cunning.

She had just made her first strike.

"Are you daring to threaten my son?" He finally spoke up, temper and fury catching with him, as he snapped out of his state of pure disbelief.

This woman...

"No. But I know that all actions have consequences, and I just hope your actions don't harm your son," she huffed.

"Shut up!" He blazed.

"No. Never again!" She didn't even wait for him to calm down, as she took quick strides towards him and did what seemed like she had been wanting to do for a long time...what she hadn't done the moment he had chosen her as his next prey.

Slap

Her soft palm collided against his hard skin, causing his head to snap to the left side.

He could have stopped it. He could have easily grabbed her hand, but he didn't. Raw emotions were flooding at the moment. Finally, they were being direct in this fight. No more facades, so more pretence, finally she was spitting out all she had held back. He wanted this confrontation. The intensity budding around them...he wanted this.

He kept staring down at her with a fumed expression, as she hotly glared up at him.

This was a fight...a full-blown, hot-blooded fight.

They had been battling for so long. Their emotions, the frictions, it was time to have a more direct and verbal confrontation.

"I loved you," she revealed, breathing hard and mad. "I had loved you so much. You were like my own hero who made me feel special and wanted. I had needed someone whom I could love, and who could love me. I was naive like that; believed in wholeheartedly giving my heart to another," she accused, the air around them growing intense and heated.

It was a whole new situation.

"My mother had tried to stop me." She then took a deep breath, trying to keep the frustration out of her voice and allowing the air to chill. "S-She had warned me about the cunning nature of street boys, but I hadn't cared" She lowered her gaze momentarily, but he kept silently staring down at her, observing her emotions.

There was so much pain, anger and regret in her tone.

She met his gaze again, both of their eyes had molten and heated emotions. "I hadn't cared about that because you had sounded so sweet, so sincere and genuine. I had truly felt your pain. It was dumb of me." The anger grew. "You made me feel like it was dumb trusting another. You might think you outsmarted me, but the truth is you just broke someone who decided to give your rotten heart a chance. Your son is pure, innocent...I hope your sins don't do to him what they did to me." Jaw clenched, she then turned around again and began walking away from him.

He was still fuming, breathing hard and furious, but he didn't stop her.

He couldn't even move, as he kept staring in her direction...feeling the weirdest form of burn settle on his shoulders. He didn't know whether to pull on his hair or punch something. It felt like she had left him feeling more suffocated than relieved, which he had expected to feel after lashing out his anger at her.

Her words had held fire.

So fearless, so direct...

She had hoped and prayed that her pain wouldn't impact his son!

She had pitied herself for loving him.

Chapter 17

E liyas

Punch *Slam* *Punch*

The punching bag shook.

With sweat gathered on his forehead, Eliyas kept on digging his fist deep into the dusty texture of the punching bag. His every punch was followed by a growl, a frustrated bark. The emotions running in his mind were driving him mad. He needed control.

Breathe...calmness...

He needed to gain control again. He strived on the sensation of control, but his tense nerves just weren't cooperating today; so out of control, so wild and intense. It had been three days since Nabeel had finally been discharged from the hospital, three days and a night since Sila had dared to fight back.

The blazing fury in her eyes, the cutting madness and fury.. .Memories were making his nostrils expand while taking heated breaths. He needed control. He needed to calm down the rage and frustration inside him.

Saud still hadn't shown up at their flat. That man hadn't been picking up calls, and Eliyas didn't know whether to drag him out from his hideout and let go of that man. Noreen loved Saud. It was disappointing thinking how careless Saud had been. Such a blunder, and now that coward was hiding somewhere.

Pity.

Feeling agitated, he threw another punch in the direction of the bag. His exercising tools had been placed right in the middle of Saud's room, and it was giving him a slight sense of satisfaction seeing how he had thrown out all of Saud's things.

Partial refund received-so much more to take back!

Knuckles clenching and tightening, with hardly any sun rays pouring into the room because of the drapes, Eliyas finally stopped to sit down and drink water from his water bottle. He had been keeping water near because of his nerves. He just couldn't keep himself calm.

He needed control. control...deep breaths in and out...

After a quick gulp of water, he placed his elbows on his knees and hung his head low. The room hardly had any lights on. It was too silent, too dark and just too provoking. It reminded him of days when he used to live in a place more smelly and vacant than this.

He had a wife that had wanted more, a newborn who made him yearn for getting filled pockets. Yet, here, with riches, his son was still suffering, his wife was dead. So many contrasts lived in one society. Rich, poor, greedy, strong...so many...

Lost in his thoughts, he frowned as his mobile phone vibrated. The police had been calling him for days, giving useless explanations. It was apparent they were trying to protect the elitist, the very notion that had made Eliyas hate that class, put them in their place.

Disgusting rich folks

However, once he picked up the call, his tired expressions turned stern, firm and cold.

Sila

The shades of the park's leaves changed. The warm breeze blew, and the sensation of watching a sinking sun hit me hard. I had been sleeping on the park bench for 3 days, eating food from a local shop that was giving away free food and just spending my days strolling in the park.

People around me were starting to notice a pattern.

Low moments...trapped in a pit; these were my emotions. There were moments when I had dared to fight, but now, there was just hollowness. Away from my family, had lost the only acquaintance I had managed to find when battling my pain, and now this...out under the streets, no real food or place to go.

I had snapped at Eliyas purely out of instincts, but now, I knew what he would do. My thoughts terrified me, yet I felt numb and in shock. Depression, loss, tragedy; they have the capacity to steal the colours of this world, turn everything so monotone, so dull.

Everything I had been through, the shock of my situation, what Eliyas was going to do next, I felt like I had been pushed to the back burner of my mind. I was just watching now. I had no control over myself and was watching the world from an outsider's view.

Numb...

How could I have allowed myself to literally end up on the streets, get snatched by some thugs at any time?

I had lived such a comfortable life. I had never even moved a muscle at my home. But somehow, I had messed up to the limit that I was now out on the streets, feeling so hungry and broken. My roommates had refused to accept me back, given I was no longer working at my own workplace and had no money. They had actually sold the few things I had owned. Maryam had already left the place.

I was alone again...

The dire situation of my situation actually had pushed me into a sense of denial, like I couldn't believe what was happening to me, but there was no waking up from this pain. No money, no food, no place to stay and no one to care. So totally lost and alone.

There were no tears felt to cry anymore.

So numb, so ruined, so crushed.

And I knew that in a few days, I would have no past to hold on to, no battle to fight against, my past would become a closed chapter, and I would have to survive this truth. This was how things were going to be now.

Getting up from the park bench, I decided to take another stroll. It was a women's park, and the ladies had already at the sight of a full moon. So many husbands had come to pick their wives from the parks.

Happy endings, a man who took care of his wife...

I was going to finally leave mine.

Under the moonlight, I walked and momentarily inhaled the feeling of when I had first fallen in love.

Falling in love was a beautiful situation.

One person can make you feel so strong, so important, and when Eliyas had stared at me and confessed his heartwarming emotions for me, it was the best feeling ever. I had been on cloud nine. Love does that. We want our demons to get accepted, for someone to truly be there, and when someone offers us that affection, we cling to it.

The erratic heartbeats, the daring sensation to fight against the world, falling in love was all that and more. And that is why betrayal hurt more. To be high up and then get slammed down on the floor. It hurt. Maybe, that is why I had been so fearful of separation. I was scared of endings. I never wanted to fall in love again.

I was worried about how this separation would further taint my image in our society but more than that, but I still missed the feeling of love. I was scared that I would actually miss it. I would feel a sense of loss, but now, I realize that it was just pointless worrying.

I had to accept my reality,

Storms brewed around, the wind hushed and withered, and I found myself mourning another one of my scars. I was a failure. I had failed so many people, and I was failing more by hurting over the concept of separation.

Dressed a bride, I had been hoping for so much happiness, and here, I was learning that love only equalled to hurt. It hurt to let go. The man I had got married to was simply a conman. But it still hurt to finally let go of a journey that I had thought would be so wonderful-so hopeful and loving.

Cold icy waves bit my skin, and I was about to scratch their stings away while miserably rubbing my shoulders when I was grabbed harshly by the arm and turned around.

"Sila," Eyebrows narrowed, jaw clenched and his son in his arms, Eliyas stood so strict and stern. So he had got the phone call. I had asked a police officer to get this message to Eliyas that I needed him to sign the papers. I couldn't say that I needed him to finally leave me because he would simply deny it. But, I was done.

I knew what he would do now, sell me, throw me away, but in my state of depression, it didn't even matter anymore. I had lost. The hurt of the tragedy was strong. There was no energy to feel and hurt anymore. I was done.

The sight of Nabeel squeezed my heart. He was sleeping with his head resting against his father's shoulder. I wonder where the mother was...why Eliyas had dragged his son here.

"You want to get a separation?" A malice smirk had appeared on his face, as he shifted his son and kept one arm around him. The other hand was still holding my arm.

Standing in the middle of the park, with the moonlight shining down on us and a pond a few feet away from us, I shivered while meeting his gaze with a frown. A monster, I was encountering a beast. A ruthless beast. He was staring down at me, and I was looking up at him. A fight between two heights.

"I do." I tugged my arm out of his grasp while staring straight into his eyes, not daring to look at Nabeel again. It hurt. It hurt so much.

"What if I don't sign the papers?" There was a hard look in his eyes, his smile mean and cruel. He was, again, in a terrible mood.

"I will drag you to court!" Temper hit me hard.

He had done so much.

The audacity of this man...I had finally decided to break myself from the shackles, and he couldn't give me that. He took my wealth, pride, friends, home, everything...it was game over now.

There was no putting in continuing the con. There was no point in him choosing to stay married to me. It made no sense. He got married to me just to con me, now that the job was done, it was time to let go of that facade. He had got what he wanted.

"Do you think I will allow that?" He raised an eyebrow knowingly, and there was that threat again. He was finally going to dump me at some dark market, take cash. But, why still bother with the charade, he could still sell me to some thugs after ending our marriage.

I blanched and paled, knowing what was to come, what happened to girls, how human trafficking worked...it was a dark road ahead, a terrifying one, where people lost their sanity, were driven mad...but the day I had chosen Eliyas, I had chosen to become a victim of the street crimes.

"Y-you c-can just let me g-go. You d-don't need to sell me." My voice shook, shiver increased, but I wanted one last fight before dealing with the consequences of my actions.

I took one step back, still keeping my eyes on him. He looked so dark and sinister under the moonlight, his expressions hidden behind shadows. I could have run, hid, but I knew that he would find me. This is how the gang life worked. There was no hiding Also, any chase would often result in a brutal hunt.

"You saved my son. I owe you now." He was crudely mocking me now, a sinister grin still present on his face. He took one step forward, causing me to take one cautious step back. I had just lashed out at this monster a few days ago, but after the adrenaline rush, I was back to trembling in his presence.

"End this already, Eliyas. You got your cash, job, everything. Now, I want nothing more to do with you, so why carry on with this charade?" I eyed him with fear, hoping someone would catch this man in the women's park.

"I won't."

"Is Nabeel's mother okay with you being married to another?" I tried to take a different route. unclenching and clenching my fists out of anxiety.

His malicious grin immediately dropped to a nasty scowl. He grabbed my arm again and pulled me forward. "Nabeel's mom is dead, so I believe she has no say in this." This man was horrible!

Dead!

Did he murder that woman?

Did he murder his wife!

Another terror hit me hard, murder...it could be, marry and kill... maybe, this was why Eliyas wasn't willing to leave me. He had plans!

"D-Did you kill her?" I stuttered, looking up at him in pure terror and worry. "A-Are you here to do t-that to me-"

Immediately, the hand holding my arm grabbed my jaw and squeezed it. "Shut up!" He sneered right in my face. I grabbed the hand on my face with both my hands, struggling for him to leave me. "If I had wanted to put a bullet in your pretty little head, I would have done it the day I dumped you."

"Then why-" I quivered. whimpering at the sight of his temper. His son was fast asleep throughout this episode.

"Why are you doing this to me?" I persisted, taking a gentle approach.

"You took me away from my home. You took my money, stole the one person I had managed to get close to throughout this process, you broke me again and again. and I want to know why? why me? Why did you choose me? What did I ever do to you?" A sense of ache and devastation entered my tone.

"Why did you choose me?" I repeated softly, vulnerability...

He kept staring harshly at me and then pushed my jaw back, finally letting go of me.

"I am not signing any papers." He moved to turn around, but this time, out of pure desperation for freedom, I grabbed his arm.

"Why are you doing this? You got what you wanted. Money, wealth, I am completely broke and abandoned now. I know you are a conman. But, please...just end this already. I don't know what I did, why my pain is so entertaining for you, but please...no more..." My tears dripped, as I then lowered my head in sheer defeat

He turned around, keeping a firm hold on Nabeel and then grabbed my jaw again. Silently, he wiped my falling tears with his thumb. For a moment, all was silent, just the sound of my broken sobs was echoing in the air.

"Why did you do it? He sighed after a minute.

"Wha-" I turned to look at him with a confused expression.

"Why did you look after Nabeel? Why did you call me?" He sounded quiet and observant.

"Because he was your son. Despite everything, I saw a connection-the son of my husband. He was so innocent and vulnerable. He needed protection."

"You should hate him." He accused, voice rough and cold.

"I should, but I don't. I don't even hate you now when I should because I don't think you deserve even that from me." My eyes narrowed in his direction. "I just don't get why you hate me so much. You have conned me, so what is the point of hating me? What did ever I do to you?"

"Nothing."

This was biting.

So there was no apparent reason for the continuation of this torture.

My knees immediately sunk to the floor and I balled up, crying in my arms, no longer bothering about how he saw my vulnerability.

This was it.

"You are so cruel, so heartless." I pulled on my hair in mad hurt. "All I ever did was love you, why couldn't you just do that? Why couldn't you just love me? Why couldn't you have just changed your ways for me? You have ruined me....you have ruined me completely, and I hope you are happy now. I hope seeing me like this thrills you. I am so alone. I am so lone all because of you!" A severe panic attack had hit me hard.

"I am so lone. What am I going to do now? What am I going to do now?"' I was rocketing back and fro, completely breaking down.

Fingers tried to push my face away from my arms, but I wasn't going to listen to anyone now. I had suppressed these emotions while depressions, and finally, those wails were bursting out. This man had ruined me, butchered my heart.

No food, no money, no job...how was I going to survive now! How was I going to get out of this?

No, no...no...

"Please," I finally looked up, as the man who had ruined me, was hovering over me with a wide-awake Nabeel. Eliyas was looking at me with so many emotions, gently stroking my hair to calm me down as he looked slightly pale at the sight of my full-blown breakdown.

"Please just spare me. Let me go."

Chapter 18

S ila

The little me had dreams, but she was lonely. I was lonely. I had a family, yet no friends. I had no friends, and it cut how despite being surrounded by my cousins, I was alone.

It is the attitude.

People can make you feel alone. Being excluded can make you feel alone. When people take you for granted, you feel alone. Some families are only connected by blood.

I was just a cousin-nothing more.

I was taken for granted, the sloppy second choice of my popular cousins who could never get over my weird habits.

'Why doesn't she party like us?'

'Why doesn't she make friends?'

I was shy, awkward and insecure. Always. I wanted to feel needed, important-just wanted, and that is what my age fellows could never give me. It got lonely, so terrifyingly lonely. Every person wants to relate, be wanted, but there are only a few open arms that offer that.

I didn't fit in, despite all my efforts, and no one tried to pull me out of my own complexes and insecurities.

No one told me that I was enough.

Eliyas did. He told me all the lies that I had wanted to hear. To be pulled out of the shadows and forced to be acknowledged. My parents adored me, and they expected a lot from me. My cousins took me for granted. They only took interest in me when a boy started to like me.

I wasn't important enough to be heard by many.

There was always something I had to give to be loved.

That is why it was so easy to drop me.

I was stuck in a rather lonely place, and Eliyas had sensed that. He had seen that as the perfect opportunity to strike. I hadn't cared about the noises that stopped me from giving my heart to a stranger. I didn't care, because one look of pure adoration, one affectionate confession, had been my ultimate weakness.

I was weak for love.

I was so weak for envying all those couples that were each others' support system.

It was just how I saw I would be finally treated important. A man by a woman's side guarantees respect in this society. A single and awkward woman is easy to ignore but not a married one. It was just how this society worked, and I hated it for doing that. I hated how I could give it all, do my best, and still my efforts would always be overshadows by pitiful gazes that wondered when I would get married.

I did...and just see how that turned out to be.

I had just been so pathetic, so desperate for love and affection.

So cold, so out of my mind that I was on the brink of turning mad. Sanity, I had always thought it was a concrete concept. No....it was completely the notion most hard to grab. The traumas and mental illnesses were tough to tackle. I had never before lost complete control. My head was in constant pain, agony...everything hurt. It was a blur in my head and I felt so trapped. I wanted to claw out of the prison of my own mind because everything hurt so much. Everything! But I couldn't.

Waking up to a darkened room, the smell of gun powder and diesel hit me hard. Rubbing my eyes, as my heartbeat raced erratically in confusion and pain, I sat up straight and found myself sitting on a dirty floor of a rather dark room. There was hardly any light and oxygen.

A jug of water had been placed beside me.

I was facing the stage of exhaustion that came after experiencing a panic attack. The cold wind made me shiver, and I spontaneously pulled up the blanket covering my legs only to come to the sudden realization that I had a blanket with me.

Where was I?

A sense of alertness finally caught up with me.

Eliyas, Nabeel...

I remember fainting because of my panic fit, but I couldn't remember what happened after that. My head was hurting. There was sorrow and tiredness weighing on my shoulders. I was in a room that was pure gravel and concrete with just a punching bag hanging in a corner from its roof.

Looking around, a strange sensation grasped me.

There had been water placed beside me. I could feel a bandage wrapped around my head.

I had been looked after.

My heartbeat started lurching out of control. I was alone in some dark room with my captor nowhere in sight. It brought back terrible memories, like the day I had been dumped on the road by my husband. The sense of deja vu was so strong and terrifying for my anxiety, that suddenly I wanted out.

Being abandoned was my new phobia.

I hated it.

A cry of fear shook my controlled nerves 'Where had Eliyas brought me?'

With every beat of my heart, the notion of horror and urgency continued filling me.

I had to get out of this place.

There was this strong level of dread...an alarming fear...experien ced

My situation seemed to turn dire and was cautioning me to be alert.

Something didn't feel right.

The man, who had ruthlessly dumped me on my wedding day, had taken care of my wounds-his acts so bizarrely made me feel like a cherished asset.

Shoot!

Rushing towards the door, the alarm signals grew intense as I found the door locked.

This wasn't happening!

Eliyas, he couldn't have finally-

No!

Pale and blanched, I began kicking the door, throwing my shoulder against it in maniac urgency. Tears had started trickling down my face as I fought against the thought of what exactly might be happening right now.

Eliyas had finally decided to sell me.

"Pleaseeee....open this door," I shrieked, digging my claws against the door and continuously shoving my shoulder against the door.

I was hyperventilating, my anxiety making it difficult to act normally and rationally.

"Eliyas! Please get me out of this place!" I was begging, pleading... "I want OUT!"

No one was answering me.

Why wasn't anyone answering me!

Why wasn't anyone telling me that everything was fine, that I wasn't been given away!

Anxiety gripped me again, as I found myself again growing hysterical-feeling the after-effects of my panic attack hit me with full force and push me on the verge of experiencing it again.

The dread was so real and was hitting me so powerfully.

"Eliyasss! Please open this door! Eliyas!" I was choking on the extreme feeling of fear.

I needed to get out. Right now!

"Eliyas..."

Memories of little me started trifling with my thoughts...reasons from where it all started.

Sheltered and protected...I had never experienced this crass side of society where no sympathy was offered. I used to the first-world hurt where people had limitations when hurting others.

I was a shy, nervous child who used to sleep with a night light on and had no idea how incredibly brutal people could be. For me, attitudes could hurt. But the real world had so many other vicious ways of hurting.

Words were just the start of destroying others.

As a child, I had a hard time expressing myself, felt shy when reaching out to others, reaching out to my mom and confessing my worries. Her love and affection made me always want to please her. I was too sheltered and protected that I would suffer when it come to conflicts.

I didn't like worrying my parents, considered my problems insignificant when I should have come forward and expressed how I felt.

I should have spoken up!

I should have confessed to my ma that I felt neglected and lonely in the shades of my cousins, that I hated being subtly pushed in the background because of my nature and felt left out during so many occasions.

I should have told her that being so thoroughly wrapped in a safe cocoon, I had never learned how to interact with people and spot danger, so was breaking in the shades. But I hadn't. And now my suppressed insecurities were hurting me in the worst ways.

Reminiscing those memories now made me feel want to give the little me a tight hug and just tell her to wisen up, to confront her shyness. She was so soft and naive; easy prey for the word. She needed more exposure.

Beneath the shelter, I had never witnessed such a crisis. I was so used to the feeling of being safeguarded from such worries that I couldn't fathom such monstrosity.

I was used to morals and the presence of conscience.

Yet, here, there was no mercy.

The warm embraces of my mom, my pa...they had never allowed me to experience this pain in my life. How could they allow me to experience it now?

Why didn't they let me come back home?

The agony grew intense.

Why hadn't they prepared me for this part of life?

"Mama...please help me," I then called out like a little child, my agony seeping into my pleas.

Even in my mother's anger, there was so much love for me.

"Baba, anyone, please get me out of this room!" I was feeling so claustrophobic.

I needed to know that Eliyas hadn't finally dumped me at some black market and cashed me in.

I needed to get out of this room!

The darkness was biting and the smell of gun powder choking my sanity.

"Please, open this door!" I kept pounding my fists against the door, dread consuming me completely.

"I want out. NOW! Please!"

A lost identity, never to be found again, a tragedy reminisced on a newspaper cover or in a brief column...I could become it all. I had read such cases, but experiences it was a whole lot different. There was fear, terror and a sense of denial.

This couldn't be happening to me.

However, as I kept pounding my fists, kicking and shoving, I heard something fall outside. I twisted the doorknob again and the door finally opened up to a dirty hallway. A rusty paddle lock was resting near the entrance of my room.

This was it!

The chance brightened the sense of hope in me and immediately dashed outside. As expected, this wasn't some normal place. As I rushed down the dark corridor, I could hear the creepy snickers of men echo in the air and smell the strong scent of gun power mixed with sweat and dirt.

A noise akin similar to the sound a gun shoot echoed from somewhere in the distance, and I kept moving, being on the verge of wailing out of extreme fear and desperation, refusing to not even let out a peep while hoping to get out of this place as soon as possible.

However, just as I rounded the corner, my hope turned into extreme terror.

Oh no!

In front of me, there was a familiar greasy man who had caught me escaping. His stance was as terrifying as I remembered it to be. The sound of his surprised and grateful chuckle chilled me to the bones.

"Oh, Eliyas finally brought you here. I think I have found the perfect gift for one of my favourite client's wives. She needs young staff for her new business."

The malicious glee behind that statement told me that this was just the start of my pain.

Eliyas

'Who would you ruin after me?'

'Who would you destroy after me?'

"Who would you continue to break with your soft tears, my sweetest flower?'

Sitting on a small couch in his room, Eliyas listened to the soft poetry playing on the radio while he lured Nabeel to sleep. His boy had been crying, so disoriented when he had seen Sila hit the floor, and now his baby was finally exhausted enough to fall asleep.

It was the love for his son that he had decided to take care of Sila. When she had latched on, begged for mercy, extreme aggression had consumed him. She had begged, pleaded, and the sight of her collapse hadn't settled well with him. The moment she had hit the floor and closed her eyes, he had wanted to jolt her awake and keep peering into her eyes.

Looking inside the window to her fragile soul gave him control.

She wanted him to leave her alone.

She wanted to end it all, and he just wanted to pull more tightly on the ropes that reigned her towards him. Her tear-filled eyes irritated him, and he wanted her to feel the same anguish and irritation.

If it wasn't for Nabeel, he would have grabbed her the shoulders and shook her hard for making him experience such unwarranted aggression and frustration.

Didn't she get that she had made the blunder of choosing him?

There weren't going to be any takebacks now.

He wouldn't allow it.

Something so soft, so fragile, having the power to crush it almost felt like an alluring addiction.

Addiction took some of his control, and that emotion irritated him more, made him want to squeeze her fragile nature and taint it black.

The desperation to remain in control had put him in a terribly foul mood.

'Your love tortures me...breaks me, when will you ever show me mercy?'

The soft strokes of the beautiful poetry continued to trifle with his temper, discomfort, and he finally decided to postpone his boxing session; punch out his aggression in silence, and visit his little patient. He had left her locked up in one of his rents rooms in the Basement.

Taking her to the hospital would have turned the experience into something more. Bringing her to his apartment would given her an insight of his life. He didn't want to give her any leverage upon she could latch on, make him appear vulnerable infront of her.

Distance was important for control.

Appearing strong and completed closed-off was vital to give one an upper hand.

'Your tears are my weakness. When will you wipe them away for me?'

Whistling to brighten his mood, Eliyas got up, placing his son in the baby carrier, and decided to finally drive towards his damsel in distress.

She needed to be thrown back on the streets.

A rustly paddle lock lying before the entrance of his rented room greeted him with a silently dangerous whisper. The room's door was flung open, and she...she was gone.

An overwhelming feeling of suffocation started choking Eliyas.

Where was she?

Nabeel was fast asleep in his life, and he was standing completely stiff. He didn't want to feel one emotion that was striking hard.

"Sila?!" He screamed, barked into the empty abyss of the room, still shocked and in denial at the sight.

Furious, he began stomping down the empty corridor with urgency and intense need. His heart was pounding fast. She had to be found. This place loved fragile women too much. He had locked her in, but apparently someone had got her out.

No one had ever before messed with his property.

How could someone had dared to mess with him this time?

Hurriedly looking around, he felt a burning sensation consume him. This situation felt akin similiar to 'Noreen' incident. No! He didn't want to go down that road.

With more urgency and sweat gathering on his forehead, he ran and searched until dusks turned into dawns, and vice versa.

One Month Later

The apartment doorbell rang.

Taking slow steps, Eliyas stepped outside with his frigid coldness more icier than ever. However, the sight before him burnt him completely to the core.

Mostly bones and mangled flesh...she laid on the ground, completely blue, broken and shattered, eyes closed, breaths hardly there.

A note had been attached on her arm.

'I heard you were looking for her. Finally decided to return her back. Enjoy!'

Chapter 19

S ila

Locked, liquified into bones that suffocate you completely...

It's chaos inside of you, and the haunting sensation is that you can't leave. You can't leave your mind that it torturing and turning you into an insane mess.

Terrifying basements, nights spent experiencing haunting pain...I found it so hard to hold on to my sanity. I felt wildly mad, almost insane, yet couldn't mutter a peep out.

I was trapped inside my own mind.

I have experienced what was purely mental torture; kept in basements with several other female prisoners, spat at by many frustrated prisoners and punished by being thrown in isolation dumpsters.

Stolen as cheap labour, I had been to work at factories and industries that smelt of lead and destroyed lungs. There was hard iron rubbing and a constant thud sound that was scarring.

Beaten for making mistakes, starved since the stronger ones managed to steal the food, I had experienced life from the point of view of a survivor-a survivor of dark market exchanges and jobs.

I have survived only because I was too weak and cried too much, which didn't go away with thorough beatings.

I had been kept underground for so long, ridden by dark corridors and enclosed spaces, that it was almost alien-like to explore normalcy all over again.

No one and nothing made sense.

I was in my mind-mute, locked and in shock.

I was a survivor.

My environment felt soft.

For me, it was just colour changes. Dark to light, cold to warm...it was so much pain that I couldn't identify a single feature of my surroundings. Faces were familiar, but I was purposely blocking them out.

It was a coping mechanism.

Block out everyone-everything that brought me pain, that hurt me, was being rejected.

Sometimes the mind does that-it rejects. In fact, sometimes, our minds turn into such stubborn organs that they refuse to ignore the pain and force us to deal with it according to their defence mechanism.

A single episode of something traumatic can be enough to trigger the stubborn side of our minds. They make us build a shield until the wounds manifest in one side of our personality.

One tries to move on, forget, suppress, everything, but the impact remains there.

The memories keep taunting us with their occurrence.

Trauma had turned me into a mindless and numb skeleton-just bone and nothing more. I couldn't speak, eat, move or even think; only clawing at the walls of my prison. I was repressing everything because the moment it started compiling on me, I wouldn't be able to bear it.

So numb, with remittances of tears rolling down my cheeks, I was spending my days just hiding inside my mind and pretending that I was still the girl who had been kept sheltered at her home, couldn't accept what had become of me, take the new version of my personality.

Bruised and battered...

Lost and terrified...

"Drink this..." Amongst the darkness, some shades of light did try to escape towards me, but that light terrified me even more. I could only stare with a blank and baffled expression as the voice spoke to me again.

"Sila, I said drink this. It will help."

I had lost the ability to do anything. It was until I tasted the chill of a cold liquid that I remained the function of taking in quick gulps.

So cool, so soothing for the constant sweat forming on my forehead.

"Good." The voice praised me, once I was done drinking the strange liquid.

Strong hands patted my head, smoothed hair away from my forehead, and left.

I simply stayed hidden in my mind.

I was so miserably, so crazily terrified.

Eliyas

Squeezed by a void...

Eliyas fed his wife some soup while managing his son over his shoulder. Each spoon he fed was punished with a vengeance and a show of aggression. He was sitting on a chair that he had pulled beside her bed.

There was this haunting need inside of him.

There was a bubble that needed to be popped. The moment he had to carry her battered form and feel her dangle so miserable. he felt fiercely furious. A petal he had meant to crush in his hands, she had been his wife, his victim...his right to enjoy her whimpering tears and observe the scars.

Don had just butchered any chances of getting a fair deal.

He would have negotiated while holding on to the reigns, but now, he knew the result, had felt the insult of being interrupted, so he wasn't willing to trade his wife for mere bucks and a chance to inhale her skirmish reaction.

Her absence had made him hunt.

Don had made an enemy out of a trader.

"Good," Eliyas now praised the one whom he had bruised, but the thrill was missing.

She was gone.

He ran his thumb over the knuckles of her fingers, which were pulling on strands of her hair, and quelled the urge that depended to press hard against her bones.

The pain was an emotion. He had wanted to squeeze and crush, experience that poetic thrill. Even the night when he had thrown her away, she had ignited and shrivelled. He had been so content with that reaction.

Now there was nothing.

Watching this side of Sila irritated him in the most discomforting ways. It had been oddly satisfying to drain emotions into her eyes, but now the skeleton of her soul was a bore to him.

Pull on her hair and yank her into reacting, he wanted to scream at her blankness, but all he could do was run his fingers through his own hair in frustration and try to keep calm. There was just so much disdain in seeing her transformed into a liquid mess.

Nabeel hadn't been making it easy by constantly making grabby hands whenever he got to see Sila.

"You are bones now. You shouldn't have been so rough with your diet," he gruffly scolded, as Sila took time with each bite.

He knew that this woman had been broken into a skeleton, but he was so horribly frustrated. His wife was messy evidence of torture and abuse.

Sila didn't say anything, just staring into one dark corner of the room, as her silhouette seemed so faint in the cover of the evening light. He had switched off all lights to create a mellow atmosphere.

"I looked for you," he then sombrely confessed after a moment, hanging his neck for a moment, and pulled his sleeping son into his arms.

He wanted to tell her that he hadn't been behind her kidnapping. Maybe, it would trigger her to feel some sort of comfort.

He hadn't looked for Shoaib, who was still cowardly hiding away, but he had tried to find her.

He needed her to know that.

She still kept staring at absolutely nothing.

His temper rose again. "Why did they do to you?" He almost screamed in frustration, but after receiving just a slight show of shakiness, he gave up on making her talk.

"Fine!" Gritting his teeth, he ran his right hand's knuckles across her cheekbone in an effort to push back her randomly fallen locks of hair that seemed to be constantly hovering over her cheeks and squeezed the urge to pull on her strands.

She didn't react, and the urge grew stronger.

Twisting a lock around his finger, he pulled on it in a rather rough manner and clenched his jaw as her emotions remained the same-bland and hidden in her mind.. His heated gaze had no impact on her

Something about her crushed form twisted his sanity.

Swaying her gaze over her face, the teary gleam in her eyes and the hollowness of her blood, he felt his raging temper tame into irritated exhaustation and decided he needed a break.

"Get better, Sila." Chucking lightly on her chin in a sombre manner, he then got up and began heading out of his room.

He laid Nabeel next to her before he left.

Somehow, he was sure that she wouldn't harm him, and he was packing all the people who needed protection in one; one big bubble that he could easily manage.

Choices; sometimes, we are so stubborn about our choice that time takes its route and pulls us in a different direction.

The day Nora had died, Eliyas had made a stern declaration to himself that he would take care of his son and make sure that his boy never experienced want. He had been strict when it came to Nabeel's needs, but he had never noticed the accidental addition of choices.

He had chosen to marry Sila.

It wasn't a necessity. In fact, he conned so many, had run from so many cities after his gigs, but she was the only one whom he had chosen to put a ring on. Her odd tenderness had a pull that he felt sinisterly amused enough to crush. He needed to marry her and crumble her softness.

She was so naive that it was insulting to see her enjoy a silver-spoon life.

She didn't deserve it.

However, today, seeing the result of his wants disappointed him. Her emptiness wasn't satisfying, and that epiphany was irritating him.

What exactly did he want?

Standing before the window of his living room, he absently stared out at the city and glared at the city life.

He had to snatch this.

He had to give his son a promising chance.

Lost in his thoughts, he snapped into his alert mode as the sweetest chuckle escaped from his room.

Nabeel was awake.

Rushing into his room, his eyes widened at the sight before him.

Cradled so warmly into a warm embrace, Nabeel was laying in Sila's arms who was looking down at him so lovingly, so motherly, sobbing upon his cheeks.

Emotions had finally been revoked.

He was shocked. He had been trying to make her feel for so long...

With each chuckle, she would draw the baby close and just hug him...like he want the balm for her heart; a woman's motherly instincts.

Pure hearts attracted all.

Agonized sobs would escape, but it was far more vibrant than blankness. And suddenly the irritation settled on Eliyas's heart vaporized. He leaned against the threshold of his room's entrance and watched in silent observation.

Nabeel was patting Sila's cheek, rubbing his head against her shoulder in affection, and she was crying while seeking comfort.

"He needs food now." Abruptly, Eliyas walked up to Sila and tugged his son out of her grasp.

She gasped in a shattered sense of loss.

Nabeel immediately started making grabby hands in the direction of the woman whose expressions were now crestfallen and miserable, but Eliyas was in no mood for such gimmicks. He wouldn't allow his son to be treated as a comforting balm.

Tossing Nabeel over his shoulder, he slightly grimaced as Sila began shrinking back into her empty mood. She had lowered her eyes, miserably picking on the blanket's thread.

Annoyed by the constant pull and push, he turned around and walked out of the room.

Nabeel was now happy to be taking a ride in his father's arms.

After preparing the feeder, Eliyas almost bite his tongue in frustration, yet he couldn't help rebuke the compulsion that had him drag his feet back towards Sila.

The sparkle in her eyes as Nabeel returned back made him bit a groan and roll his eyes. She was NOT allowed to get attached to his son; yet nonetheless, he, once again, sat on the chair placed beside her bed and began feeding his son.

She was solely focused on Nabeel.

It almost seemed like his son was some kind of a threat pulling her out of her chaotic mind prison. Without him, she would be tugged right back.

"I will get you some milk, too."

Again, she didn't respond.

Frustrated, Eliyas ran one hand down his face and ruffled up his hair. He couldn't stay cooped up and deal with this when he had so much to do. He had to go back to work, and he had to somehow make sure that his son was being taken care of while he worked.

His muscles needed stretching, and he needed to get rid of the irritation that seemed to be igniting his temper fuse so frequently these days. He wasn't a man of reaction; never impulsive or driven by moments.

He had always been so in control.

Today, he wasn't.

Chapter 20

Eliyas

She was still the same. His wife, the woman whom he had refused to give divorce, was still in parallels with her trauma, and Eliyas couldn't help but spend days assisting her.

Spending nights with a loosened collar, he would do his office work in the lounge and then try to block out the whimpers of the battered woman whose screams would reach each corner of his apartment.

Hearing her now scream once again made him frown, close his laptop and get up with a grunt.

"You need to go to sleep now." Casually jutting into her room, he leaned against the threshold of his room and raised an eyebrow at the sight of her sitting upright. She was softly crying into the curled palm of her hands.

Thankfully, Nabeel was sleeping on the living room's couch.

Eliyas had shifted his son's sleeping spot since the night Sila had decided to scream out her trauma instead of keeping it bottled in.

"Where is Nabeel?" A quiet cry echoed through her whimpers. Her gaze was lowered to her folded hands. She had a need in her tone; the desperation to hold his son.

"Sleeping...as you should be. It is three in the morning," he sighed, eyeing her pitiful form snuggled so miserably in a blanket.

"I want to go back to my home." She miserably began pleading, looking at him with watery eyes.

Terribly heartbroken.

Her expressions caught Eliyas off-guard, hiccuping him out of his casual stance.

"Go back to sleep..." He turned around to walk out of the room again.

He was exhausted, too tired for it all.

"I miss my ma." Resigned, stuck in nostalgia...she seemed to sound like a lonely child that simply wanted the embrace of her mother.

"Do you think she will want you back after you chose to run away with me?" An eyebrow quirked, and he swiftly turned back to stare at her with a taunting frown while folding his arms in a stern manner.

It was too late, too frustrating and just too bitter.

"No." The teeniest resignation peeped out.

"But I miss her. I hurt her." An anguished sob entered her tone. "I am suffering because I hurt my parents, and now, I just want to go back to her. Please..." She had started full-blown crying now, hiding her face in the palm of her arms.

She was an absolute crumble, a mess.

"I want to go back home! I want to, but I cannot...I can't go back. This is my punishment. I don't want to stay like this anymore." Verging towards hysteria...

So much pain and anguish escaping out of her heart.

Eliyas was staring with a slightly disturbed and uncomfortable expression, trying to run his hands through his hair while giving up on doing anything.

She would have a fit, often.

However, her next words widened his eyes in shock.

'I don't want to die like this. I cannot be this alone. I can't."

Sheer broken and miserable...

His tired stance shifted, and he pushed up his shoulders to stand straight.

He had heard the same words before, held the same crumbles before.

Nabeel's mother had pled the same.

Bleeding on the ground before him, shot by the folks on the road...it was part of living on the streets. She had got influenced and morphed herself into an easy target.

"I don't wanna die...please." She had sounded so meek, so scared, hand grabbing his ankle.

He had moved back and looked away with a retired look; angry, hurt and not really surprised.

It was just too disappointing, felt like an obvious defeat.

"I told you so. You knew this would happen." His words had been curt, almost cold because of suppressed anger, emotions cut back, and his voice was quiet.

His shoulders were slumped down.

Her pained sobs immediately echoed in the air, mixed with a gurgle.

"I am so sorry, Eliyas. I am just so sorry."

"I know."

"Our son won't have me."

"He will have me."

He knew there was no point in taking her to a safe place. The people who had shot her would be back at any moment to clean up their mess and take care of the evidence.

He was too selfish to stick around, take her, and risk the chance of going back to his son.

Gang Rings erased all pieces of evidence and all witnesses.

His wife had made a mistake.

He had warned her, thought she was clever enough to avoid such doom since they both had grown on the streets, but she wasn't.

She was a fool, a tactless con artist.

Her sob had then echoed until they faded away.

He had turned his back towards the raging storm in the distance. It was only until the pelleting down of the rain, that he bent down with a look of a hint of sadness, a sense of loss, and carefully closed her lids with a gentle touch of his knuckles.

Bent before her on one knee, he had caressed away the blood mashed on her neck and remembered light days when it felt good having a partner by his side.

She was sweet support.

Celebrations, which included coffee mugs and cheap Chinese food, after each successive con, racing, riding together on his bike after midnight and just firing bullets in the air in a show of rebellion; they had been a good pair.

"Goodbye," he had whispered.

She had just been too reckless.

Her death was considered a usual on the roads-nothing out of usual.

Snapping out of his gloom and doom memories, Eliyas moved his gaze back to Sila while feeling tempered by her attitude.

It was disgusting.

Born with a silver spoon, her collapse was an insult to him. To break so easily when she had suffered bruised and cuts, but never a bullet to her skin.

Rich brat!

Somehow, the image of her face replacing his late's wife's on the road forced a sudden sharp pang to his heart. That image unsettled him. She was too cultured and poised to be treated as street disposal. Tough roads didn't suit her. It was like forcing two parallels together.

"You chose this." He simply shrugged, walking Sila break into pieces. "You chose me.

Immediately her watery eyes reached him with the clearest gleam, "Not anymore. I just want to go back home. I miss my family. I want it all back...please..."

Another fit, another wave of anxiety-induced tears...

Sighing, he turned around, only to stop when he heard a sudden strangled tone escape into her tone.

"Sila?" He turned back, eyes widened in shock.

"I cannot breathe!" She had started hyperventilating, moving her hands around her neck. "I cannot breathe."

She had started to claw.

"Shoot!" Rushing up to her, he watched as something shifted, and she fell back on her bed.

Eyes closed, her stance still shaking, she had fainted.

102 degrees...

Hands folded before him, he was sitting on a one-seater and watching Sila still fast asleep because of being overdosed on medicines.

Her fever was hardly going away, and he had pushed a seater beside her bed.

A crumbled rose...a poetic thrill to experience, a possessive growl of control, but the spark of experiencing a sadistic appease had dimmed when the petals had simply started wilting instead of twirling in impact.

Three days were gone, and her fever just seemed to be staying.

Dark circles had formed under his eyes. He was still working from home, and he hardly got time to punch out his aggression and exhaustion.

Night times were tricky because sometimes, Sila would start to hallucinate in her dreams.

Like now...

Her limbs had started moving, her eyes had started leaking tears, and she had started mumbling desperate pleas in her tone.

'Please...no! Don't leave me here! Don't leave me here!"

She had started madly thrashing.

Immediately, he sprung into action.

"Sila, wake up! Wake up!" Pushing her by the arm, scolding her back into consciousness, he watched her with aggression, as her eyes finally opened to meet his gaze with a hint of fear and grogginess.

"Not another one of these!" He bared his teeth in irritation. "I will throw you out if you ruin sleeping hours like this!"

Her grogginess quickly cleared up into awareness.

"You did this to me..." She started retorting in mad shivering while hiccuping, but his sharp glare was quick to shut her up.

"Nabeel is asleep! Don't you dare let out another peep and disturb his sleep!" His voice was harsh and stern.

He was going to have none of this.

"I hate you so much! You are disgusting. I hate the day I chose to marry you! I-I wish I could just go back home. I-!"

"And I have heard you say that a million times!" He was fed up. "You stole from your family to run away with me! Some love you have for them, princess! Now stop with this brattiness and let me check your temperature." He stood tall before her.

Roughly rubbing his hands against his forehead, before she could back away from him, he frowned as the heat bit his palm.

She still had a high fever.

"You are burning up." He simply remarked all signs of temper and irritation vanishing.

He was simply exhausted again.

It was silent again.

Collapsing down on his seat, he sighed, closed his eyes and momentarily pinched the bridge of his nose to regain control.

"Listen," he opened his eyes to see her now silently crying on her folded knees.

She looked up and met his gaze in a miserable manner.

"This is not going to work."

Her breath hitched.

"My son needs consistency. He likes you, and we need to get rid of this constant back and forth, so tell me what do you need me to do for you to get better?"

She didn't speak, so he decided to propose the option.

"Okay, so this is what we will do...we will develop normalcy. I will go to work, take Nabeel with me, and when I will return home, you will be ready with our dinner. We will dine together. It will make you feel less alone, and Nabeel will feel good. Capisce?"

She still didn't respond, but he had made up his mind.

"Capisce." He reiterated, answering his own question.

Yawning, he then got up and stretched to destress the pent-up aggression and annoyance.

It had been a long day...

With Saud still on the roads, on the run, it was strange returning back to normalcy. He had no clue where Saud still was, and he was meaning to have a word with Don.

What happened to Sila was still suspense...but he knew that it was Don sealing a deal that he had yet to make.

Snatching instead of signing was a direct show of undermining one's authority, and with Saud gone, Eliyas knew that there would be words around, people wondering who had the better business hand.

No one enjoyed a weak trade or a powerless businessman.

Where people could snatch, why would they trade and make deals...?

Sila had been on his property before she was taken. She had been his prey, his choice and his deal to be bargained. Don had misstepped. It was an indirect threat, a violation, and if he let that go, then the respect and reputation he had gained on the streets would be put in jeopardy.

Showing yourself as an easy target on the streets was a blunder.

Allowing others to make a fool out of you is a dangerous choice.

One has to maintain the upper hand, keep a crass grip and school those who dare question your position.

Street laws mostly revolved around earned respect and the survival of the fittest principle.

Making his mind to sort out things in the morning, Eliyas strode out of his room and decided to prepare a cup of tea for himself.

Sila was left sniffing behind.

The city life was shouting outside, and Eliyas needed some calm and control to deal with the unorganized thoughts in his mind.

He liked to plan, control and think out his next moves.

Right now, he was just thinking about returning back to having a routine in his life.

Chapter 21

E liyas

Something domestic started happening...

For the first time in his life, Eliyas found himself living a city boy's life. It was always settling and relaxing to get a routine.

He would spend his days in his office, attending meetings with skyscrapers peering through windows and returning home to find Sila playing the role of a seasoned wife.

It was clear she wanted distraction and stability.

She would wear washed clothes, arms folded and looking desperate for normalcy.

She had morphed into an obedient kitchen wife quipped with knives and an apron.

It was a change.

To have substance to return back to felt like a change.

She had accepted his offer.

He would throw his briefcase on the couch, and wash his face and hands, while she would simply serve food and settle down to eat.

Dining together built a routine.

He knew this was needed.

He had spent most of his life busy dealing on the streets and scooping prey for easy money. It was nice living the life of a white-collar job man with a wife and a child.

Normalcy took away suspicion and gained defence.

The clocking of even hours, the screech of silver against plates and the sweat of the day formed on foreheads, it was normal.

Every day, after dealing with exhaustion and long hours behind his laptop, he would return back and settle down on one of the chairs in his kitchen. She would sit before him, on the opposite side of the kitchen island.

Nabeel would be placed in his baby chair.

The heat emitting from the stove, the homecooked food and the comforting silence would do so much. So much...that he had actually started looking forward to returning back to his apartment after work

She won't say much.

She hardly reacted, but it seemed like she also was tired of their bickering encounters. Fighting regularly had drained her.

Tears and gloom had exhausted her, and she looked like she wanted to fill her brain up with some work.

It was good.

He was relieved that she had chosen to comply instead of just being a tiring duty.

He needed to relax.

Sitting on his chair, he was in a good mood as he sliced pieces of his steak. She was looking down and eating chicken salad, both arms on the kitchen island.

Both of them were keeping quiet.

Nabeel had fallen asleep on the way back home, so he was napping in his newly-bought cot.

A good mood equalled a mood to talk.

"This steak is delicious. Your cooking skills are quite impressive. I never knew that," he chuckled in amusement, relaxing back in her seat.

She didn't respond, simply shifting pieces of lettuce around with her fork.

His smile immediately turned into a bored frown.

Sighing, he began chewing on the juicy meat while resting his chin on the palm of his left hand and staring at the show before him.

He quirked an eyebrow at the sight of her mousy ways.

Tiny bites, moving her fork around the bowl and hiding hiccups of loneliness in her mood, she looked too wimpish.

Sweet twilight was peering into the room from the window behind her back.

Neon lights were glittering in a fancy way.

Sweet!

"Sometimes, I find it extremely hard to believe that a girl, like you, decided to elope." A rather nasty smile appeared on his face, his face leaning on his palm.

Her movements stopped immediately.

"So how did you do it?" He now folded his hands and placed his chin on them, grin wide and malicious.

He was bored but in a good mood.

Her reaction felt like good entertainment.

"I tend to trust easily." Her voice was so quiet, tiny, and reserved, still hunched over her food.

She curled a lock behind her ear in an awkward manner and returned back to eating.

She was speaking for the sake of ending the conversation, her gaze never moving away from her food.

"Silly..." He chastised her with a nonchalant shrug of the shoulders and a good-natured smile, taking another bite of his steak.

She had been behaving these days. She had accepted that this was needed to ensure that Nabeel felt safe and comfortable.

Good!

"Indeed. One has to be an utter fool to love you."

Her remark immediately made him straighten up, good mood and humour vaporizing.

Love...

She had spoken without daring to look up.

"You never loved me. What you did was more for yourself..." he spoke in a cold voice, not tolerating such confessions.

His unamused gaze shifted between his plate and her face.

She had sounded so childish and foolish.

His city bride had simply chosen him because she wanted to experience the thrill of rebelling against her elite norms and falling for a dirty street biker.

He sure taught her what it felt like to live on the streets.

The bliss was real.

"I know." Her tiny confession caught him off-guard.

She had squeezed into the comfort of her chair.

Despite his remark, he had enjoyed the ego boast that cherished the emotion of being able to fool the heart of an obedient elite.

Her emotions for him felt like power.

"See..." A nasty smile on his face appeared again.

He chuckled in a rather patronizing manner and took a bigger bite of meat.

Control...

"You were so easy. It was extremely entertaining," he started adding, purposely goading, anything to get back the ego rush.

"I wasn't that easy if you had to marry me to get cash."

Bitten words left him speechless again, his mocking smirk immediately turning into a frown.

"So why do it?"

"What?" He raised a confused eyebrow, sporting a scowl.

Her attitude was starting to test his patience.

"Why marry me?" Her fiery gaze only met his for a second, before lowering back to her food. She seemed to be working on controlling her temper, her grip around her fork had tightened.

"What the heck! Are you serious? Are you still trying to fish for...something? Because I don't want you to hurt your pretty head by still thinking-"

"I don't want anything to do with you!" Her hands slammed against the table, causing him to snarl in disapproval, his eyes narrowed in a disgruntled way.

"I just want to go home! You are a sick person. You are horrible, and I just want to get out of this horrible mess! I am scarred, destroyed and miserable! I want to go home!"

"News flash; you ditched them for me. I am pretty sure your family won't be ready to welcome back a little thief, so sit down and be grateful I am being generous enough to babysit my son and enjoy my food! I can easily throw you out if this continues." His eyes blazed with irritation and annoyance, as his gaze sternly gestured her to sit down.

He was in no mood to deal with her routine tantrum. Again!

She made a choice. She needed to accept it like a big girl. Her mousiness and delicate ways were getting on his nerves.

If Nabeel wasn't so besotted by her-

"So why are you?" Reluctantly, she did sit down, but the anger and rebellion were still clear in her eyes. She didn't move her gaze away from him, as her voice cracked with a hidden sob.

"Why am I, what?" He bit back a bark, fuming that she was still daring to continue with this conversation.

"Why are you not throwing me out? Nabeel is young. He will forget me." she goaded, though, she immediately looked like she wanted to take the words back.

She didn't want to be thrown out.

Eliyas could see right through her bluff.

A tiny smirk appeared on his face.

"Should I throw you out?" He teased, resting both arms on the table. He leaned forward to enjoy the sight of her breath hitching in fear.

She immediately lowered her head and began eating her food.

Not another peep escaped.

"Good. Stay like this from now onwards." His smirk was mocking and bitter, as he kept his gaze slightly bulged out, fixated on her lowered head in a patronizing manner, and his arms folded on the table.

Ensuring that she remained docile, he was about to return back to looking at his own plate with a satisfied smirk on his face when she suddenly stood up without looking up at him.

"I will eat my food with Nabeel. Excuse me." Her tone was wobbly, teary, as she simply pushed in her chair and sped out of the kitchen.

Yet, another tantrum of hers...

"Sila!" He stood up too, throwing back his chair in the process.

He stormed out, wanting to put her in her place, and rushed towards his bedroom. She had now locked herself in it in a hurry.

"OPEN THE DOOR! NOW!" Hitting his pounds furiously against the door, he barked out loud, briefly eyeing his son still sleeping in the cot placed in the living room.

He hated how this episode was going to wake up his son.

This woman...

"I told you I will eat with Nabeel. Please..." She seemed on the verge of crying, sounding beyond terrified.

"Get out! NOW!" He persisted, hating how she had the audacity to lock his room's door.

"Please..." She was begging for mercy,

"I am going to get my keys..."

"Okay, okay..." With her whimpers shaky and audible, she hurriedly opened the door and sank down on the floor, covering her head in fright.

He stood before her with a deep frown.

Seeing her tremble, shake and protect herself from him made him sigh and then sit before her.

"I am not going to hit you." He rolled his eyes, annoyed that she had tightened her grip around her head.

"And I am not going to throw you out..." He continued after a moment, moving to push her arms away.

She immediately flinched back and looked up with red eyes, sitting on her heels.

"I wish you would." She bit back, looking ashamed of showing vulnerability before him. "I wish you threw me out, so I didn't have to depend on you for anything. I hate that I need your place. I hate that Nabeel is your son. I want to go back home."

She was goading him again, spewing the words of a pampered princess who wasn't getting her way.

He gripped her arms in a merciless way.

"Then go and beg there instead of being a brat here! But they don't want you back, do they?" He taunted, watching as extreme hurt flashed in her eyes.

"No, they don't," she spoke quietly, lowering her head, but he wasn't done with her yet.

Gripping her chin, he pulled her face up to meet his gaze again.

"So, stop fighting this," he spoke sternly. "My son needs normalcy. He is the reason I even bothered with someone from the city. You can make this easy on yourself, or just continue testing my patience, your choice. But I really don't think city folks are too forgiving towards dirty thieves."

"My family doesn't want me back. But you do? You want a dirty thief to keep Nabeel happy?" She countered instead in a mocking manner.

Before he could respond, a loud wail echoed in the air.

Shoot!

Nabeel was awake.

However, before Eliyas could even get up, Sila was up on her feet and rushing out of the room. She had Nabeel in the cradle of her arms when Eliyas walked out of her room.

Suddenly, the woman, who was having a meltdown, had morphed into a gentle mother for Nabeel. She was stroking his hair and rubbing his back in comfort. Nabeel had started laughing in joy instead of screaming his lungs out.

It was a strange sight.

Eliyas leaned against the threshold of his bedroom, watching the scene with the weirdest thought in his mind.

She had asked if he needed her here.

The question irritated him so much.

The way she phrased the question had been so frustrating. She had mocked his decision to let her take care of his son. She was trying to get the upper hand. He felt furious by the attempt, yet he still couldn't throw her out.

She was making Nabeel happy.

His lack of full control of the situation was messing with his organized calm.

Chapter 22

S ila

Wide eyes peered deep into my eyes. I could hear the hurried heartbeat of a man who had made me experience the merciless taste of deception. He stood tall and urgent, snatching my palm and holding it tightly.

"Here, take this card and some cash. I will meet you in a few days. Don't run away."

My eyes narrowed in fierce chance.

There was no longer any need to hold one.

This was my opportunity to break his hold on my dreams and strengths. "I want you to give me div-"

"Ask me that when we meet next time." For a moment, his eyes softened, and he hovered until his friend growled in urgency.

"Eliyas! Hurry! We need to go!"

"I NEED TO GRAB MY STASH, FIRST!" He barked back and then turn towards me, pulling up right-hand palm-first before him.

"Don't leave this place. Also, don't call anyone. I WILL get to know." He glared harshly, slamming stacks of money and a card into my hand.

I curled my hand around the offered support. He wanted me to pay his bills and keep his place running. I could help but frown at his audacity.

The nerve...

He was absolutely crazy and insane. Yet, I was more focused on the strangest twists of events rolling before me. Maybe it was too late. Maybe I was so wrecked to enjoy any positives, but I couldn't help glaring back at my husband with a newfound sense of defiance and fury.

This man was going to escape.

After destroying so many, this man and his friend were going to take off.

His friend had shown up this morning, claiming the city police were trying to track down the duo. The man had started with so many desperate apologies and reasons for disappearing and then claimed how Jasmine had the authorities trace his steps all the way to the city.

My ears had heated up at the words!

It was humiliating to be reminded, again and again, that I was just another name on Eliyas's list. I was an absolute fool...the most naive person, falling for the most basic con. It was so shameful and crushing.

However, I couldn't linger on that emotion for long because I then saw my husband and his buddy preparing to leave. They were going to take Nabeel along!

Nooo...

I didn't know how many times they had done this, how many times they had hid the road to hide from the police, but I couldn't let Nabeel be a part of this. He was sleeping in his cot, so unaware of the harsh ways of the world.

I wanted to scoop the victim, just like me, and make a run for it.

I couldn't.

Eliyas was the father.

He was taking his son on this hit-and-run detour.

I felt terribly heartbroken.

I didn't know who this Jasmine was. I didn't know how she managed to get so far, but I wanted to applaud this woman for her fight back. She was making this criminal sweat bullet and going back into hiding. Eliyas probably wouldn't get captured, since this duck and cover seemed like a usual pattern of his lifestyle, but I saw this as an opportunity

Maybe, just maybe, this Jasmine was going to be Eliyas's mistake. She was going to finally get the police to catch him and throw him behind bars. It was a liberating thought, just imagining Eliyas regretting all he had done to me, to others, and grovelling for mercy.

I wanted to see him beg, plead..thrown back on the streets where he had pushed me as his replacement. He needed to be slammed with his biker boy status again, so he would be reminded of whom he truly was.

Gosh, I so badly wanted to see this man thrown off his throne and dumped into dirt!

That sight would be so healing!

Yet, I was so devastated and frustrated to see Eliyas escaping before my eyes and being able to do nothing about it.

I couldn't stop him.

He had me trapped in a situation where all I could do was watch, be his compliance.

I wanted to play my part in putting this criminal down, be the hero of my story, yet I knew that by the time police would catch up, Eliyas and his friend would be long gone into hiding, and I would simply not be spared when Eliyas decided to come out of hiding and found out that I had tried to aid the police.

He had fear and what-ifs nailed into my roots.

I couldn't mess around with the possibilities.

Men, like Eliyas, were gruesome with their revenge schemes. Once returned, he would go for the kill, dump me somewhere, and escape to loot others. I had fallen into such horrible hands where survival was just temporary.

I was one snap away from being sad news.

My helpless devastated me.

I needed to help the police catch this criminal.

The man who had clawed out my everything needed to be put behind bars. I couldn't let him live a remorseless life.

I couldn't.

I was devastated!

"What am I supposed to do while you are gone?" I spoke in an irritated manner, wincing back as he grabbed my chin with a smirk on his face.

"Miss me." He simply winked, sporting an amused expression.

I stepped back in disgust, narrowing my gaze harshly.

"I hope you get caught."

Immediately, his teasing mood dropped into a stern frown.

"Don't go anywhere, or else..." He stepped forward to intimidate me, glaring deep into my eyes to get his point.

"I hope you get everything that is coming for you..." I huffed instead, looking away while folding my arms, trying to appear nonchalant.

My heartbeat was racing fast. I was pretending to act tough, but I was also nervous about what was going to happen next, what was going to happen to me. I didn't want to be left alone when I was still traumatised by my kidnapping episode. I didn't want to deal with being on my own when dangerous mafias were already aware of my presence.

Just the mere thought of being caught again...I didn't know how I was going to deal with it all and deal with hurting for Nabeel.

The thought made me want to wrap my arms around myself.

I just wanted to go back to my home now.

I was so tired of being this entire mess.

"Repeat these words again when I come back." A threat, a warning, he wanted to say more, and before I could retaliate, I heard sirens echoing in the air.

My eyes lit up in anticipation and shock.

Could it be?

The police were here?

"Dudeeeee!" Eliyas's friend barked out in urgency, and I saw Eliyas quickly moving away from me, scooping Nabeel from the cot and rushing to walk out of the door.

The sight of a sleeping Nabeel going along crushed me.

My heart raced in anxiety. I kept staring wide-eyed, pale and desperately looking for a way to save Nabeel. Yet, it was all pointless as I could only watch in extreme despair as my innocent baby disappeared out of my sight and straight into the streets. I had no idea when I was going to see him again. I had no idea when I was going to hug him again, and that thought made me breathe hard.

My poor Nabeel...he wasn't at fault for his father's actions, and he was going to suffer so much.

The thought of him suffering and begging for me made me feel so lonely.

I had done nothing for a boy who was a victim--just like me.

I couldn't protect a baby who saw me as his world.

It tortured me to think how poisoned he was going to be, how rough things might get from my young...

It was a heartbreaking emotion to see the one innocent soul, that had been my anchor in this traumatic experience, was about to become a victim of the crime world.

Life on the run...

Nabeel didn't deserve that.

I was left oddly exhausted, breathless and empty as I witnessed darkness settle back into my surround, the sound of sirens fading away, and neon light lit in the background.

Numbed yet overwhelmed by all that had happened in mere minutes, shocked that I was finally going to get some time away from Eliyas, I couldn't help but stare blankly at the apartment door.

I was alone.

I was going to be on my own...for some time.

Time can be a gift.

Time can make us sink down on our feet in joy and get baffled by its unpredictable nature. It was only a week after miserable gnawing on nails and wondering about what was next when I called the strangest call on a phone left behind for me--by Eliyas.

Eliyas and his friend had been caught. The police raided some underground storage place and caught Eliyas dealing with some guns. I burst into tears the moment I was told that man, who had butchered my heart, my confidence...my esteem...and drained me onto the brutal streets was finally going to get what he deserved.

I was in shock.

"Seriously?" I held the phone tightly in my hands and dropped myself down on my bed.

It was night time.

I had kept only one lamp light lit in my room.

"Yes." I had no idea who the caller was. She didn't sound as if she was from the authorities.

I wondered if it was a trap, if this was Eliyas testing me...

"Who are you?" I then inquired, hiding the scare in my voice while chewing on my thumbnail, desperately praying for the hinted lie to turn into truth. My gaze was anxiously swaying across the floor.

"One of the workers who helped con you. I want to take my out, too."

My eyes widened in shock.

"What-"

"Check the news if you don't believe me." The woman was stern, sounded honest.

Hesitant, I did a search on the web and was stunned to find an article telling how they were able to raid an underground basement and capture two wanted criminals.

"What on earth!" I covered my face!

It was unbelievable.

The man who had seemed so solid, soo strong...he had been caught! It had to be some type of game or strategy. Imprisoning

Eliyas couldn't have been that easy. He had links with human traffickers and gangs. He was an expert at escaping the law--that is how he seemed to be surviving

I was hearing lies, seeing lies...

"Why are you telling me this?" I bit back, feeling lost in my emotions.

"Need a clean slate. There are many women, like me, who are getting paid to be his hired actors. Some of them want a bigger cut. I want his wife to know the truth while I pay my way out of this business." I could hear a lonely ache covered by a serious attitude.

It broke me, too.

So many lives, Eliyas had crushed so many, and apparently, he was finally caught.

Caught!

The man who had left in the middle of the streets in my bridal dress was finally caught!

Tears began leaking in shock!

My dimly lit surroundings were making this situation seem unreal and insane.

It was such a bittersweet experience.

I couldn't believe that it was going to end.

Jasmine, I hadn't met that woman, but she had been a legit surprise in my life. I believed Eliyas could never get caught by one of his victims. He seemed so careful, so cunning and careful with his ways, so powerful, but I guess it is the arrogance of criminals that can be their downfall.

Any moment can catch you.

Jasmine was influential enough to become Eliyas's mistake.

It was still so surprising how this woman had got the police to trace him down.

I was witnessing the consequence of thumbing down others, and I was truly so astonished.

"The police might already be on their way go get you, too. Do you want to run?" The woman offered.

I just didn't know what to think or say...while holding in a gasp.

"I am 28 years old. I have a small family that lives in Karachi. I live here with my brothers in a one-story house. I admit my job isn't anything out of ordinary, but I work as an evening salesperson at a mobile shop. If you say yes, I promise I will keep you happy."

"I am sorry...

I felt light, so bewildered, as I allowed memories to weigh down on me and words on the call to coax me into giving.

It had been difficult.

It had been so tough.

The cracks all over my heart scream just how much Eliyas broke me. It was too late for me now. The damage done had been permanent. I couldn't go back to my home anyhow, but this was the start of receiving my balm.

Tears started trickling down my cheeks. My limbs drooped down in an exhausted mess. I kept nodding, revealing and shaking so much, embracing the shock of the news, while thinking about another tragedy echoing in the distance.

"No, but where is Nabeel" I spoke in a whisper, already devastated about what was going to happen to that boy. I didn't want to ask this question. I was terrified of what I might hear, what might make me regret letting him go so much.

I wanted Nabeel back in my arms.

He wasn't going to be scarred just because his father was a terrible man.

"I heard the police have handed the baby over to the child protection program for the time being."

"Oh," I lowered my gaze to the creases on my clothes.

The authorities won't let me keep him. I had no job, no permanents.

So much mess, so many lives tainted, because of one man... Nabeel, Maryam, Me...one man had been able to cause so much destruction. It was honestly depressing. And I had decided that I wasn't going to allow him any cutbacks.

When the police would arrive, I was going to testify against him.

Chapter 23

Eliyas

It was temporary.

This trap was simply a rich girl throwing a tantrum because she couldn't get the street biker boy to become her clean and polished 'yes' man. He hated such spoiled brats, hated Jasmine for thinking she would be able to punish him for her bruised ego.

She was just crazy mad because she loved a dirty boy and couldn't make him fall for her. These city girls, from the pampered streets, felt insulted by rejections, and Eliyas had butchered her bratty attitude by not only dumping her--but using her in the worst ways.

He had no idea how she had managed to track him down, how she had got the audacity to gloat at the sight of him dumped into a police car...but he was going to put her in her place.

Once he got out, once Shoaib got some mighty loan sharks from the basement and Don to make some calls, he would be out again. And this time, he would make sure the preppy and scared-of-breaking-their-nails princesses truly understood what happened when they mingled with people from the streets.

Both Jasmine...and Sila.

His wife...the title made his jaw tighten in a fury. She had been the ultimate posh wannabe and was testifying against him.

He would strangle her, ring his palms around her neck and throttle her. He would crush her foolish decision to go against him when he had shown her mercy and given her a place to stay. He knew there wasn't any room to show softness in this part of the streets, knew his wife needed to be coined in for money, but he had been having too much fun messing up with his timid prey.

Now he was fuming at her, glaring, as he stood before the podium while watching her take the stand, look at her palms and then nervously confess to how he had hurt her.

Both his hands were tightly curled around the stand.

Somehow, he was madder at her than Jasmine-that rat!

"He conned me into marrying him. I left my house...for him." Her voice cracked...was too quiet, conveniently avoiding his gaze, and he tried his best to not sneer in disgust.

He hadn't forced anyone.

She couldn't even meet his gaze when telling her the truth!

Liar!

Her, Jasmine...these weak women were the ones looking for adventure and trying out their luck with plucking and cleaning a man who was below their status quo. He simply taught them a lesson about what it was truly like living on the streets.

"Okay. Thank you for coming forward," smiled the prosecutor.

Sila had the audacity to accept his smile.

His gaze narrowed into malice.

Pathetic snitch...bailing at the first chance!

He would deal with her once he was done with this.

He kept staring at her, as she mistakenly met his gaze and squirmed in discomfort.

'Oh'...he suppressed a menacing smile, digging into the wood while gritting his teeth.

He would definitely crave a grin on her face if he hadn't.

She didn't have the guts to look at him, yet was so sneakily stabbing him in the back.

She should just wait for what he was about to do.

Just wait!

The judge then asked Sila to step down, and she simply walked passed him without sparing him another look. He kept hotly glaring in her direction until she sat down.

That pathetic rat! So poised, so confident only when knowing she could hide behind guards...

Breathing hard, he momentarily looked down to control his temper and focused back on the court session.

He had to stay calm and composed.

His baby boy needed him. His Nabeel was the sole reason why he was stopping himself from jumping the stadium and reminding his dearest wife what exactly he was capable of. She had mistaken his calm as a weakness.

He would show her exactly what kind of man she had married, what happened when someone messed with the future of his child.

His first couple of days behind bars had been maddening. He had spent most of his time banging the cell bars in fury and making sure that Nabeel went nowhere. His baby boy was allowed to be kept close to him with the help of a policeman who belonged to his base.

He wouldn't let anyone touch his baby boy...

All he did was for his baby's future...

He wouldn't allow snobs to mess with it.

And today, he was going to make sure to get the wanted verdict from the judge, grab his son and return back to deal with all those who had put him in this position. He had long forgiven Shoaib. That boy hadn't acted out of the ordinary.

It was every man for himself on the streets.

It was these women who weren't getting the hint!

"Okay." The judge now folded his hands, making Eliyas look at the judge with a strained look. "I have reached a verdict," he announced.

Eliyas's breath hitched. He quickly eyed his boy sitting in a pram held by an officer, gulped a hint of nervousness, and then looked back at the judge.

The room had turned silent, all eyes on the judge.

"The court, hereby, announces that Mr Eliyas is sentenced to five years in prison. His wealth will be confiscated by the state and distributed among the woman whom he looted."

Eliyas's jaw dropped in shock.

What?

"His son will be handed over to CPP for now and will get registered for the adoption program-" The judge continued, unperturbed by just what he was saying, "-if Mr Eliyas is unable to become a functional part of society after five years. Mrs Eliyas will not be handed over custody of Nabeel Eliyas since she doesn't have a proper setup to raise a child."

"Mr Eliyas will be eligible to apply for parole after 3 years."

Eliyas's eyes rounded in extreme disbelief, horror and fury!

He snapped forward, still holding onto the podium.

No! This was wrong!

The judge wasn't supposed to spit this junk. Don or any of the loansharks were to intrude.

Where was the real verdict?!

Why did the judge want a bullet in his head?---because that is exactly what was going to happen once he got hold of a phone.

Panicked, he desperately began looking at his audience, swaying his gaze for some kind of detour, his backup...Anyone from the basement would be furious that a man holding so many secrets was caught by the police. They would want to interfere.

He wouldn't allow the court to cage him up while the rich brats fanned dollars.

His son...Nabeel...he wouldn't let anyone touch him!

The court was up and cheering now, getting on his nerves and suffocating him even more.

He needed his control back!

Everyone was on their feet.

The judge had started collecting his notes while calling in the guards, and the court printer had been awakened to print out the decision.

This was foolish!

Jasmine and Sila were standing up and hugging...in the first row.

Fury gripped him hard!

These women were giving him their back. They were thinking that they could get away with this. They couldn't!

These people were fools if they believed he would just comply with their order and allow his son to get dumped in some dirty place. He had only bothered with cunning, disgustingly pampered women because he wanted to win a rich and comfortable life for his son.

This was all for him!

He wasn't going to allow anyone to mess it up.

These women didn't know what was an adventure for them, was the reality for many.

He would kill before allowing such women to be his doom.

Shoaib was to be trialled next.

This had to stop!

Immediately!

Quickly looking at his baby boy sleeping in the pram, he eyed the distracted crowd, the slow approach of the guard and then nodded his head in a calculative manner.

Everyone had underestimated him here.

Everyone had taken a street survivor lightly.

He was going to go for the kill!

Quickly, he sprang forward and pulled a distracted guard standing by his podium in a headlock. The gun was pulled out easily. It was a part of his training.

He had been a part of many gang wars to not be able to ambush one person.

"I WILL SHOOT!" He barked, looking wildly at the crowd and watching with satisfaction as the room instantly stilled into horrified silence.

Everyone was staring at him in horror.

The guard was breathing hard in stress, trying to get himself freed from the grip, but Eliyas simply pushed his gun deeper into the man's temple and sneered at the crowd.

"I WILL KILL IF YOU DON"T MY SON AND ME TO LEAVE...RIGHT NOW!" He wildly threatened, ignoring the sweat forming on the forehead of the scared guard.

"Mr Eliyas...you are threatening an armed man in a full court. The penalty of such a crime is-"

"SHUT UP!" H growled madly, tugging on the guard's neck in a harsh manner. "I WILL SHOOT!"

"And we will make sure your son never gets to see you." The judge was calm, too calm.

He moved his deadly gaze to a police officer who was standing by Nabeel's pram. The man picked his son up and began stroking his curls.

Nabeel woke up with a smile.

The smile was toothy and gurgly..,

Eliyas felt his gaze hitch in a sense of deep grief. His son didn't deserve this. His son didn't deserve him as a father. His boy deserved better so much better...he wanted so much for his Nabeel--a dream that his boy never remained this side of his pa's life.

Distracted by the most common weakness, emotions, Eliyas was shocked as someone injected something in his neck and ambushed him to the ground!

It was the guard he had been holding in a headlock. His distraction allowed the man to strike.

Immediately, the courtroom was full of screams.

The shrieks were intense and violent, yet all, he could do was close his eyes in an extremely weak manner and call out to his son.

"Nabeel..." His voice hardly reached out to anyone.

He had finally been taken down.

1 year later

"She is a complete loser. She fails her classes and gets so serious when Sobiya is just messing with her. No one in her class really likes her. She is too quiet and skirmish...but she is so loaded," Shoaib chuckled. He was leaning against the alley wall that was on the way to their town's extremely popular women's college.

Eliyas simply stood next to him with a hidden smirk with folded hands. He side-eyed his friend and returned back to quietly observing the crowd to look for his next victim.

"Point her out to me." He simply ordered, stroking his chin.

"Her...There she is...this is who Sobiya was talking about."

A young girl with red on her cheeks, eyes towards the floor...she looked too awkward in the crowd, too shy in her stance. She was walking with some other girls. But he was sure whom Sobiya had meant.

The signs were obvious...

She was too delicate, seemed too sheltered and too tiny in contrast to her surroundings.

It had been a sunny day. He had been smiling, planning to put on a show of charms, but then, suddenly there were so many greys.

The clouds jolted.

She looked up, something he didn't remember her doing, and she looked straight into his eyes with a terrified look.

Suddenly, he felt as if he was standing in the alleyway, burning away...his smug expression instantly morphed into a deep frown.

He turned completely towards her, taking a step forward.

"Sila..." He reached out a hand, wanting her to shade him because he felt like only she could.

"Sila..." He desperately screamed again, watching as she began running away. She didn't listen.

She didn't take away the exhaustion resting on his shoulders.

Eliyas woke up in a sweaty mess, rolling around in his cell bed. A memory had once again merged with a nightmare for him.

He sat up straight, placing his hands beside him and began look-ing at the moon peering down at him from the cell's window with a tired expression, breathing hard. He had no cellmates. Shoaib had been clever enough to find a way out. And he...he was just feeling silent.

They say the collapses are always the hardest.

He was still in denial, still shocked, and somehow, terribly broken by the mere fact that his son had been given away to a family. He had been able to hide for so long. His imprisonment seemed like an impossible reality, yet it had happened.

How?

He had no idea. He had been so careful and serious. Was it relaxing into the city life that was his downfall? Probably.

He had been reckless.

He had lost Nabeel, and now there was no point in fighting for a fair chance at anything.

There comes a storm in life that is too powerful to be denied, and it jolts everything. Breaks everything.

He had a strong spine that was no longer interested in fighting and trying . He wasn't able to protect his Nabeel and was getting nightmares about Sila. That woman was irritatingly being a consis-tent occurrence in his dreams, and he hated the emotions he would be feeling in those dreams--reaching out for her, hating her fearful eyes---disgusting!

He hated that woman for what she had done to him.

Her fantasy of living a street life, well, this was the real street life! Deaths, murders, separations and living off looted wealth, because no sophisticated society spat in the direction of the poor, were the real truth of street life.

This was how street bikers lived! And she was going to go scathed free, hehe-ing her way back to normalcy while he got to rust away behind bars while knowing his son was probably getting hurt by some foster family.

His son was getting damaged, and he felt too destroyed to even think about what was happening to his baby boy.

He had been told that his boy was happy, loved..but he knew what happened to the babies of criminals...

He didn't want to even go there, feel that part of his heart where he missed Nabeel.

His supressed truth had broken him, silenced him down into an exhausted mess.

Now, he was simply staring at the moonlight with his heart racing as a consequence of his memory-turned-nightmare.

"Why marry me?" Her pouty expressions, her red cheeks and her hot gaze...

He had made a huge mistake to allow her to stay with him. He should have dumped her on the roads and never reached the moment of dreaming of her fearful look.

"Indeed. One has to be an utter fool to love you."

He shivered at the audacity of her declaration and hated how this memory was quickening his heartbeat.

He hated being miserably trapped in a cell, feeling scorched over his son's pain, staring at the moon with strange loneliness, and allowing his dreams to mess with his heart.

He did not care about Sila...he didn't want to think about the woman who took away the one thing he ever bothered about-his son.

Chapter 24

Eliyas

6 months later (1 year+6 months after Eliyas's Arrest)

Life can get cold. It can turn into a camp settled at a crossroad meant to shelter a damaged man. Eliyas would wake up as a poor man and shift against emotions that had sprung on him in the worst of times.

Crush...

His constant dreams, one face reappearing...it was the most horrible time to get a crush, especially when that crush was a horrible choice.

No! He had battled hard to understand what was going on, to even give into the idea of crushing...

But every night, he would dream of her face. Every day, he would feel his heartbeat thud erratically and his forehead sweat in confusion.

At first, he tried to convince himself that he was simply confused, that it meant nothing but missing the easy life of control and set routines.

Yet, he missed her.

His butchered personality, beaten-out ego and defeat were giving him all kinds of feels.

He felt like a shell of his biker-boy personality...the machoness, the alpha attitude who was too good for rich brats...

He couldn't crush on the woman who was from the favoured side of the streets. She had everything until she was a fool to let it all go. She was a completely dumb prey, so ungrateful to live on silver spoons while he would rot away, searching through the trash for sellable products to help his son sleep with a full stomach at night.

She didn't deserve to be admired, missed...yet in insolation, she was all who was bombarding his dreams.

Sila...

"I heard you have a wife and a child. Must be hard to let them go. Did your wife file for divorce already?" A jail thug, with muscles able to intimidate everyone but him, sat next to him during the lunch break.

"No." Taking a spoonful of green gravy, Eliyas spoke with a stoic, almost bored, expression.

Nothing interested him nowadays.

Nothing...

"Oh, she must love you a lot. I don't know why you are in here, but you seem tough. Wanna be on my side? We can help each other during jail fights. I am seriously in the mood to bash a few here. During midnight mayhem hours, we can roughen up some of these with our fists and get them to work for us here! It will make things so much more amusing, here!"

"I don't love her." Eliyas snapped back in annoyance, still stuck on the love part.

The man smirked, leaving his tray, and looking at Eliyas with added interest. "Oh, I am already entertained. I never mentioned you loving her. So we have a sentimental guy in here! Trust me, feels will make you an easy target, Men in here like beating up loverboys!"

"I have lived on the streets long enough to deal with these men." Eliyas glared back, intimidating the man down into a cowering fool. "Also, my wife was just one of the many rich girls who helped me get some easy cash." An arrogant smirk appeared on his face, happy to be reminded of how far he had been able to pull Sila along, grateful to be reminded that his dreams meant nothing to him.

That poor girl...

"You married one of your victims? Wow! Good game. She must have been tough if she got you to marry her in order to scam her. Impressive!"

Eliyas's eyebrow narrowed in thought.

No! She wasn't tough at all.

She was tiny and so gullible.

In fact, she would have given him cash to make wedding preparations. She was that big of a fool.

He had to give her his title.

He needed that control.

Now, sitting alone in his cell, Eliyas was wondering why he had needed this control with her when he hadn't needed this with Jasmine or any other victim of his. He was thinking all such wrong thoughts at the worst time.

He wasn't supposed to analyze anything or think about the women who had put him here, but he was just feeling so beaten down today that the absence of his ego was making room for so much. He remembered her happy smile the day he married her, her looking up at her with so much tenderness...

Suddenly, that image had him breathless.

Crush...

It was so wrong to feel anything but disgust for his wife. But he was learning he didn't hate her. It was never about the hate. It was about being captured and intrigued. It was about how powerful she made him feel, how fragile she seemed...

It....he hated the pounding sensation of his heart and the reddening of his cheeks...

She was doing a number on him. Her absence and his broken ego were doing a number on him, and he had no idea how to deal with it.

He was battling with so much. The prison isolation was driving him crazy. He wasn't like those rich folks, born with the luxury to love. The basement and streets would chew up boys who turned into sobbing poets for women. Women were to either be traded in or become battered wives whose jobs were to nod and obey. Not be treated as a crush!

He needed to get out. He needed to go back to normalcy.

The moonlight was reminding him of her eyes.

But he couldn't. There was no one terrified enough to bail him out.

Time and too much emptiness were making him accept his defeat.

He was losing control, thinking too much and giving in to his feelings.

He was missing her, his son...

Today, he had to make another decision to help ensure his son was safe.

Sila

Every day started off so beautifully, so majestically now because I had learned the important lesson of never letting words reach me. I had settled down in my life with a good job, secured by the card left for me by Eliyas, and a flat to enact as my shelter.

It had been so hard to feel beautiful again, to feel whole again, until I found myself being pulled down again.

I wanted Nabeel's custody.

That boy had been my home. My baby boy.

I couldn't go back to my old home. They didn't need me. Nabeel did. That baby was hurting, learning, just as I did, and I had to take him back from the authorities. I had to. That was my weakness.

Eliyas was exploiting it, now.

I was visiting him to finally end my chapter with him, and get my closure, because I believed seeing him turned into a weak grovelling mess would give me satisfaction.

The man who took so much from my life, I needed to see him bleed. I needed to see him regret, so I could finally put close a depressing chapter of my life. However, the sight of a broken man clinging to his prison bars as he looked at me with desperate eyes was the biggest lesson of my life.

The haughty man, who had terrorised me, belittled my existence into his toy, who seemed like he could never break, was clenching the bars and looking at me with a maniac and haunted expression.

I was standing a few steps away from his prison bars. He was tightly pressed against the bars, envying my freedom and silently begging for me to help him. A man once so strong, now so weak, I felt tears brim my eyes.

"Eliyas," There was darkness surrounding us.

Words can't bring us down, but this guy had been enough to bring me so down in life.

He had pulled me down in his toxic mess, making me hate myself, too.

"I will give you what you want once I get out. Just please...take care of Nabeel till my punishment ends." He was gulping to keep his voice from cracking, his fists wrapped so tightly around the bars for support.

He was still taller than me.

I still had to look up.

The biggest irony of my life was that man, who had shown me no sympathy, no mercy, had reached a point in his life where he was pleading with me to show his mercy.

It depressed me. It hurt me so much that this man had caused me so much irreversible damage and ruined me, he was only breaking down when I had lost everything.

It had been game over for me.

His damaged and troubled soul had dragged me down, too. With him.

"You-"

"I miss you. I don't know how it happened. But I am telling you. I need you. I think I am in I-love with you. Yes, I love you," His gaze turned wild, frantic.

I could hear the beating of his heart.

Those loud confused beats...they sounded so panicked.

Immediately, my shoulders slumped back in so much hurt, disgust and disappointment,

Lies, his messed up mind, jail trauma...he wasn't going to drag me again with the word 'love.' I was beautiful in so many ways. I wasn't going to let this man get to me again, make a fool out of me again.

"You took it all, Eliyas." I looked up with tear-brimmed eyes, gaze so furious and fiery, and my hands clenched into fists.

"I don't have much more to give. If you think you can use me again to step up towards a better life, I am sorry..." I stepped forward, trying to meet up with his height with my temper.

His breath hitched, as he quietly stared back at me with shame. He was eyeing the closing distance with an uncertain and tortured expression.

"But don't you ever try to manipulate with the word 'love' again..." My brows narrowed in firm warning.

He gulped again. "I don't know how it happened. This crush, it happened," he moved back to clench his hair while his voice dropped down, "it happened. It wasn't supposed to. But it did." He looked back at me again. "And now I know it makes no sense to you now. But I-I just want you to keep Nabeel till I get back, and then I will give you what you want." He clenched his prison bars again.

"I am sorry."

"Please stay..."

"I can't. You know how this was going to be. Deep down, I know you knew that this wasn't meant to be. I am sorry. For what it is worth, conning you has crushed me too, but as I have always said...not everyone gets what they want. Goodbye, princess.

"You really did see me as just another pathetic girl madly in love with you, didn't you, Eliyas?" I sighed in a defeated tone, looking down at the gravel.

"Sila-"

"You always saw me as an easy game, didn't you? It was fun laughing behind my back, cracking over how easy it was to rope in a college girl acting so desperate for love. I was always so easy, so desperate for attention, and you knew just how to make that work for you, didn't you? I was dumb and such easy prey, believing your lies with so much naivety, and that is why you still believe you can manipulate me again, isn't it?"

"I-"

"I wasn't finished!" I snapped. He looked shocked by my reaction, taking a hesitant step away from the bars as I hovered closer.

Grabbing the bar cells, I gritted my teeth in extreme fury. "You believe you can again make a complete fool out of me and use me because you believe I am dumb enough to know any better, and you know what, Eliyas...You were and are right." I nearly screamed, glaring deep into his eyes. "I was a fool. I was so desperate and pathetic for love that I made the terrible mistake of sparing a dirty criminal like you a minute of my life. I was far beyond your league. I was too good for you. You knew that, too. Now, I will never stoop down to that level. I will take care of your son till you are allowed to take him again and free me. I will raise your boy because I am still a fool. I am still your get-rich-again plan, but I will never let you make a fool out of another girl. I will never allow you to morph another girl into me; a naive fool, a stepping stone for you!"

Determined and flared up, I simply turned back and began taking firm steps away from him.

I was breathing hard.

This man was disgusting, so selfish and cruel.

I would never lower myself to his level again.

"Sila...please..not like this. Please..." His cracked voice, tears...

I never witnessed those. I never witnessed this man crying, breaking...I had wanted to see this for so long. I had wanted to hear his tortured cries when he stood so arrogantly above me while I was lowered down to wipe the ground beneath his feet.

I had waited for his back to bend when he had broken my spine to ease his ego.

Now, I wasn't going to allow him to bring me down.

With each step I moved forward, I was leaving my past behind.

Never again was I going to let this man make me feel pathetic and anything less than valuable.

Never again!

Chapter 25

Eliyas

His sentence had ended. And now he was standing before a window, leaning against his bike with his arms folded in an emotion of deep sorrow.

His wife and son were inside a small ground-floor apartment.

He could see their silhouettes, feel the breeze of the evening tease his senses and remind him of all he had lost in life...because of his own blunders.

His Nabeel was so big now, so grown up. He had missed so much. The first day to school, the first fallen tooth, the first bicycle ride, the first word...

A sigh escaped straight from his heart, as his shoulders remained slumped.

The progress from the top to bottom was something he never believed he would experience in his life. He had been almost arrogant, too confident, and now there was a foreign sensation of defeat resting on his shoulders.

It was almost surreal, an out-of-mind feel to understand that he wasn't as powerful as he had assumed himself to be.

He never knew he would morph into a shaky man, but five years had been enough to pull him down to his knees. He felt different now, quieter...more reasonable. Power had been such a vague concept, and he had finally experienced what it was like to not be in control.

The man (who once had no qualms about breaking hearts and never believed he could be on the other side of want) was finally realizing his macho attitude had been extremely foolish immaturity.

He had hated the silver-attuned folks, believed they deserved to be pulled down from their pedestals-it was his right to pull them down, and got the biggest shock of his life when he got thrown off his high horse and told that he wasn't someone to be sympathized with.

It was an odd feeling.

Being humbled so bluntly by life was an odd sensation. His situation was even more ironic because he had fallen for another. The tough man who considered himself so powerful and in control was now experiencing the pain of unrequited love. The odds, the irony...the way he had been humbled...

Chuckling softly at how he had been turned into a complete joke, he stared at the silhouettes formed on thin white curtains and watched as they happily roamed in the kitchen.

His family...his...but he had been on the defensive for so long that they no longer considered him as theirs. He had spent his life wanting the best for Nabeel, loving his boy, and now his boy had already learned to be happy without him.

"I am sorry...' He spoke into the hollows of the twilight, but the regrets were all so real, as his lashes lowered to his cheeks in plain exhaustion.

It had been a long and hard battle.

A war against his status, the streets, and eventually he had to accept that it was what it was. He was a poor street boy grown among poverty and trash. He was weak and dirty. He had been fighting against himself for so long.

Today, he wanted to fight for someone else. The always-so-selfish him was no longer the man he used to be five years ago. His arrogance, pride...everything had been turned into a sheer form of mockery for him.

Undermining Jasmine's pain, Sila's pain had led him to this...

He hadn't understood the consequences of leaving behind scorned hearts. He had been so confident about his power and strength. Five years of isolation and thinking had scorched him into understanding how ignorant he had been.

The silhouettes moved before his eyes, and his wife picked up his son and swayed in absolute joy. The duo was making a cake.

The image pricked the tears in his eyes.

Suddenly, with the roads vacant and the silent air morphing into wind, he flexed back against his bike, placing his palms behind him, on both sides of the bikes, and then closed his eyes.

He imagined been in there, with his family.

Stepping in the flat, and being welcomed by the sight of Sila rushing towards him with a gentle smile.

"Eliyas!"

"Papa!" His boy was there, too.

His happy grin was so surprised and elated. He imagined throwing his suitcase away, taking off his wrist watch to pocket in finally, as a spoon full of tonight's dinner was pushed towards his mouth.

Even in his imagination, he didn't want to be a street biker. Maybe, it was a complex. White-collar jobs were treated with dignification and admiration.

"I made rice pudding!" The sparkle in his wife's eyes, as she welcomed him in the most homely way...

"Yum!" He imagined chuckling, grinning, suddenly feeling so refreshed even after a long day of work and playfully huffing as Nabeel jumped into his arms.

"Thank you! I made it especially for you!"

So sweet, the smile on face so homely...

He imagined his eyes softening in adoration.

It was heart-squeezingly wholesome, but that wasn't his reality.

He opened his eyes and looked at the moving silhouttes again.

This was his reality.

From afar, with regrets and a broken pride, this was his truth. The boy from a streets confusing so much with everything and losing it all in the process.

He had learned his lesson.

He had experienced the excruciating pain while locked in cells, developed the habit of spilling his words out on dirty pages instead of beating them out, and today, he was here to do exactly that.

Since last year, he had started to work on a note, something, he wanted to give to Sila when he would get out of prison. There had been so many thoughts, regrets, realization, so many explanations, so much, and today, he was ready to give those notes to the person they had been meant for.

He wasn't going to confront her.

Not yet.

But he was going to make sure she got to read about his days in the prison.

Hearing the clouds now rubble above his head, he then pulled out a brown envelope from his leather jacket and decided to move up Sila's apartment door.

Nervously shuffling his hair, he bent down and then pushed the packet under the door sill.

His heavy was heavy. The wind had picked up again, and it was roaring just like the storm inside his heart.

Feeling dejected and so weak, he then turned around and went back to his bike.

"Please...just one more chance..." Eyeing the silhouettes once again, he closed his eyes and kicked started his bike.

He had to return back to the streets...again.

Sila

Unpredictable.

Rocks, rolls and solid grounds...I had experiences, repented and learned. And today, I was finally considering myself stable.

It took me five years of healing, mending and accepting to move on from the phase of hurting because of my choices and learning that I didn't have to keep punishing myself for my blunders.

I still didn't go back to my family because of embarrassment, small and regret, and today, I had finally managed to stand on two feet and build my own family.

Nabeel was my family.

The only favour Eliyas had done me was leave me a company card. Near the outskirts of the town, I applied, got the job of an amateur writer because they knew Eliyas, got some experience, and then switched jobs to work at another firm that searched for experience, worked hard and finally was able to rent a small apartment where Nabeel and I could live in comfort.

The progress was surreal.

Burying myself in work seemed like an absolute opportunity to try and heal from the trauma of becoming a victim of street crimes, yet I knew I had to balance it all for Nabeel. My baby. He needed healing, too.

My boy had suffered so much because of his father, and I wanted him to experience what it was like to have an actual family. It was him and I, hurt by the same man, healing together. He had started calling me the best mama, and I loved him so much for it. His dad had been a complete disappointment, and I used to worry about not being strong enough to help him get over his wounds. But my Nabeel was a strong boy.

Unlike his father, my Nabeel was so considerate, empathetic and kind.

"Nabeel! No!" I now laughed, as Nabeel continued feasting on the cake batter.

We both made cake on family night.

"But I cannot stop, mama. It is too good!" He honestly sounded so troubled and helpless, making me chuckle in amusement.

"But how will we bake a cake if you eat all the batter!"

"You can make some more." Cute.

He always did that, and I never had the heart to stop him. My boy was just too adorable. Yet today, my leniency at the sight of him sitting on the kitchen island and scooping up cake batter from the bowl had more to do with me finding him adorable. Today, I was also terrified.

His papa was getting out of prison.

I had received the call, just this morning.

I had Nabeel's custody, but I also knew how aggressive Eliyas was.

What if he stole Nabeel from me? What if he simply took off with my boy?

I was so worried and scared, and I had taken a day off from work simply to find an alternative where I could make sure Nabeel never left my sight. A babysitter, a nanny...the office daycare centre...I didn't know what to do.

I had already called his school and told them to never let anyone else but I to pick him up. I had already called the police station and talked to them about my concerns, but as of this moment, they had told me to relax, and that my address was secure and kept private.

There was nothing much they could do for me, and I was scared. So terribly scared.

"Nabeel, tell me my phone number again." I then asked in a sombre tone, working to prepare a new batter. I had been doing this with him since morning, making sure he remembered all the rules.

"Mama, I already told youuu..." He whined, busily smudging the chocolate all across his face.

"I know. But do you promise you will go nowhere without your teacher's permission?"

"Yes. I promise."

"Even if Khalid asks you to?"

"Yessss...promise." He took another mouth full, making me smile.

"That is not good for your tummy, my super boy. Go and wash your face now. I will get your cake done and bake you some cookies too."

"Yay!" He immediately got off the counter and rushed outside. "Love you, mama."

He was so energetic, and it made me super happy to think that I had been able to keep negativity out of his life.

"Love you, too!" I yelled after him and went back to preparing the batter.

However, just as I had made the batter and was about to pour it into the baking utensil, I heard Nabeel shout from the living room.

"Mama, there is something on the floor."

My eyebrows narrowed in confusion.

"What?" Cleaning my hands on a handkerchief, I moved out of the kitchen and saw Nabeel standing before our locked main door with a brown envelope in his hands.

A feel of alarm hit me.

Here, I had been so cautious about his safety, and my boy was opening doors under my nose.

"Nabeel, did you open the door without my permission?" I narrowed my brows in disapproval, feeling my heartbeat race with anxiety.

"No, mama. I found it on the floor next to the door." He immediately shook his head and walked up to me, moving the big envelope towards me.

I frowned.

"Okay, my super boy. Now go and wash your face as I told you. I will see what this is." Giving him a soft smile, I ruffled his hair and patted his head to get the message across.

"Okay." He immediately sped away, vrooming like a car across the floor.

He was my greatest gift.

Shaking my head at his endearing antics, I returned my attention back to the envelope in my hands and stared at it in confusion.

Someone had probably pushed it inside from underneath the door. But who?

A strange feeling of dread and denial of something I already knew was making my heartbeat race fast.

Who?

Why?

Hopefully, not...not this soon...

However, just as I pulled open the envelope and looked inside, my face blanched in horror.

Oh no!

Epilogue

S ila

Breathing can sometimes turn out to be the loneliest experience, especially on frigid days. Summer was around me, but all I could feel was the frigid breeze of cold regrets and sorrow.

I was in a mourning mood.

The tragedies of the past, the regrets...

Sitting in my office alone, I was sifting through files and realizing one crucial emotion, one that I had never built to courage to face before...

Forgiveness.

My eyes tightly closed in despair, as I inhaled an agonized breath of air and then reopened my eyes to tiredly look at the envelope resting in the middle of my office desk. My office room was small, white tilted and had a wall-length window (situated behind my desk) that peered at the blue, smoky sky.

I was miles above the ground, and I felt as if I had climbed this high to escape from everything that my heart didn't want to accept.

I didn't want to forgive myself.

Despite finally moving on with my life, accepting my scars and heartbreak as an experience, forgiving myself was the one thing I could never do. I held a grudge against my stupidity, my stubbornness to become an easy target.

I had made it too easy for people like Eliyas to prey on my heart,

My choices, even my arrogance about believing a guy could go crazy over me...they had been my biggest mistakes, and I hated how much I had lost because of my dumb choices.

People, like Eliyas, were in numbers. They hurt and ruined, lurked in corners for a chance, and I, being ungrateful for my comfort, had decided to foolishly jump straight into a common trap. That was something I could never forgive myself for, and if I couldn't forgive myself, how could I ever forgive anyone else?

Tears of suppressed hurt and pain gathered in my head that mourned the loss of a girl who was madly sure about being a princess meant to be rescued by a prince charming, and I leaned back against my office chair, staring at the white ceiling with despair.

There was sunlight flooding my room...a desperate need to focus on something that kept me going was stressing my mind.

Nabeel...my baby boy...

I had to focus on him. I had to remind myself that I was a mother to a little boy who had been deceived by a loved one, too. We had a common factor in our lives; the same man whose selfishness had ruined so much for us, and I needed to save my son from becoming as scarred as me.

He was still so young, still had hope...

And if Eliyas took that hope away from him, I would never be able to forgive myself. It was my way of healing. If I could save Nabeel from his father's mess, I would feel as if I had rescued myself, too.

I was desperate.

I needed severe rescuing.

I missed my home and my loved ones who had probably already disowned me...and if I truly needed to keep out the extreme feeling of loneliness and abandonment, I had to keep working on the feels that made me feel part of a family where the bonds were willing to fight for each other.

Nabeel and I only had each other in this place.

We couldn't let Eliyas take that away.

I couldn't allow Eliyas to take away yet another source of happiness from me.

The tension, the anxiety, the fear...it was now starting to give me a headache.

Quickly taking a sip of coffee from my coffee mug placed on the right corner of my table, I then straightened up and decided to do what I had been dreading throughout the morning. I had made extra calls to Nabeel's school to let them know not to allow anyone to come and even meet Nabeel.

I had even called the police station to let them know where I would be today, in case Eliyas decided to act funny.

Now, it was time to face the situation head-on.

Sighing, I piled up my work files on the left side of my table, so I had enough room to relax and look at the envelope meant for me.

Placing both arms on the desk, I then grabbed the envelope with both hands, feeling a trembling sensation jolt my strength, and opened it up.

My Sila,

I am missing you.

I almost crumbled this paper at the audacity...this disgraceful, spineless and selfish man...

I close my eyes, and you are there. I look around, and I feel breathless because of your absence. I am dreaming about you, being told about how lucky I was to be loved so beautifully. And I know this is my punishment.

Remembering you now...

I am a broken man. And I hate how I had to break down to accept that I was actually living the biggest irony in my life.

To want someone I had always promised to hate.

I am a complete idiot, and that doesn't change anything.

I still miss you.

I don't want to. I don't know why it is happening...why now when women from the cities have always disgusted me so much, when I hate the rich for being so entitled and throwing scraps for the people on the muddy side. I don't want to be a lover...yours to keep, but why is missing you making so much sense?

I cannot get rid of my racing heartbeats, the memories of that day you stunned me while dressed up as my bride...you looked soft, cute, small...easy. I had to marry you. This is my why. You asked me so many times, and I am understanding that now.

I was a complete fool to deny that you were something that was so out of my control.

Now I know I have done too much to ever earn your feelings back for me.

It is one of my biggest regrets...my biggest loss.

To have something and lose it when you finally want it...

I know you have been a good mom to my Nabeel.

So I will never hurt you or my son by forcing you to stay.

Instead, I will win you and my son back....even if I never get the chance to cherish the feeling of being your whole world again.

The loose pages placed in the envelope are all the moments I jotted down while obsessing over you in my jail, being told by my jail mates how lucky I was for having a wife and child outside.

I hope you read them all. I hope you understand what happened to me in prison, how many times I breathed after dreaming about you...

Your husband.

Lies...all he ever spoke were lies, but even his truth was no better.

A gulp of tears and misery hitched up my throat.

Easiest; that is why I had always rebelled. The weak feelings were where it all started. So easily used and suppressed, I had chosen Eliyas to feel heard and cherished. Something I looked for amongst my cousins. I had chosen to trust love because it had made me feel like I was finally something to be earned.

And yet again, Eliyas believed he could pull me towards him by manipulating me. He thought I was gullible enough to buy it all again, would go back for his scrapes and learn that he was just abusing the word love for me.

I hated how I had once been all that and more...

It aggravated me so much to even remember those moments of being dressed up as a bride for him. For such obvious lies, I had made a complete fool of myself. I had made a complete drama out of myself for someone whose toxic nature was all his own doing.

I should never have become part of his drama. I should never have let a damaged man with a dirty heart soil my happiness, too.

I hurt my family for someone who envied my life.

I knew what this letter and 'missing you' was all about. A man out of his depth, who had experienced losing it all...this was a momentary reaction towards dealing with a dented ego.

People with suppressed goodness never did what Eliyas did to me.

Good hearts never propelled the ruination of another.

Eliyas was simply a rotten, highly complex and selfish criminal who was now dealing with the shame of getting clobbered at the prison. People who returned back from prison either craved dark retribution or had finally learned their lesson.

Eliyas was probably a lost aggressor who was bleeding with the humiliation of feeling powerless among the prison walls. He wanted to have control again. Me again, so he could once again feel good about himself, but this time, I wasn't going to be any man's punching bag.

In fact, I was never going to be an easy target for anyone.

Emotional manipulation; I was once such an easy target of people manipulating me by telling me what I wanted to hear. They fed me lies after capturing my desperation for affection, and I was finally done with giving just so many chances to those who knew exactly what they were doing.

I couldn't forgive myself, and now I was going to make people witness how deadly and lethal my hate was.

No more melting at soft words and patiently waiting for changes that just never came...

I was going to make sure Eliyas knew he handed over his son to me, and now he had to fight, beg, and plead to even get a glimpse of my boy. He owed me more, too. Permanent freedom, but I would not let that become my weakness.

I would speak up, fight in the court...

But an abuser, like Eliyas, was never going to be able to manipulate me by dangling the word 'love' before me again.

I would never stand that again...never get used in search of lies that just weren't meant for me.

Crumpling up the letter in mad fury, I was just about to toss it away when I heard a knock on my door.

"Sila, Ma'am is not in the office. I am sending the man we called in to interview for the new intern post to your office. You can check his credentials and his sample works while we wait for ma'am."

Shoot!

I was so not in the mood to deal with anyone or anything at the moment. Also, I never dealt with taking interviews before. He? This office was female-centric, so why was a he even being hired? Probably to help around in the IT department.

Ugh!...to talk and listen...

However, before I could say anything, my office door was softly knocked.

I heaved a sigh of exhaustion, placing Eliyas's envelope in the compartment below my desk.

"Come in..." I sat up straight, dutifully looking at the door, as I folded my arms on top of my desk.

To smile in moments when I felt so low and quiet...when I felt like silently mourning my mistakes and regret...

"Good Morning, Ma'am,"

My breath hitched, my skin paled...my strong posture melted into a crumble of emotions...as locks of hair instantly escaped my well-set and covered style.

In life, we dream about so much. We dream of a chance, some retribution, and sometimes, we do circle back. People who hurt us so miserably, so badly...sometimes, we are presented with the chance to have an upper hand and trace back the wounds that crushed us.

Standing before me was the man who destroyed so much for me; made me the loneliest person, and suddenly, life had given me the chance to make or break him. This could be a game or a con (words he had promised in his letter) but the look of hesitance, desperation and destruction told me I had a starving man before me who really did need a job.

Eliyas was nervously scratching the nape of his neck, giving me a side-loped grin.

Disgust filled me.

I could send him away.

I could refuse, say no...scream and hyperventilate my opinion.

I was already breathless, but I knew I had to be quick with my choices.

I could either wither way or enjoy this delicious reversal of power and use it to make sure Nabeel never had to deal with his messed-up dad.

Immediately my expression turned cold and reserved.

"Morning, take a seat."